A.E.G.I.S. TALES

A Retro Pulp Anthology
Vol. 2

FIRST EDITION
ISBN: 979-8-9861181-3-0
Additional Editing by Raechelle Downing
Cover art & design by Todd Downing

Deep7 Press is a subsidiary of Despot Media, LLC
1214 Woods Rd SE Port Orchard, WA 98366 USA
WWW.DEEP7.COM

To my fellow authors and creatives—
Welcome to the sandbox once again!

Let's have some fun.

- Todd Downing
Summer, 2022

CONTENTS

Introduction
by Trish Heinrich

I'll never forget the first time I fell in love with pulp adventure.

I was a little girl, sitting enthralled as the screen before me flashed images of danger, mystery, and adventure. The jungle was thick, humid. I could almost feel it on my skin as I watched the hero trudge through it. I was breathless with anticipation as the daring archaeologist braved booby traps, betrayal, and poison darts to get his treasure. For about two hours, my little brain was soaked to the brim with scenes of fisticuffs, underground tombs, and romance.

Of course, I'm speaking of Indiana Jones.

But when I went to look for more adventure stories, I was more than a little bummed to discover that many of the women in them lacked agency and were treated as damsels in distress and objects of desire. To be fair, Karen Allen set a high and unusual bar for women in pulp adventure stories, but I didn't realize that at the time. I just lowered my expectation that the genre would offer me the female heroes I was craving.

Then Todd Downing's AEGIS universe came along. Suddenly, there were women kicking butt and taking names. Women who were evil. Women who were brave. Women who were adventurers *and* mothers.

Writing in his world I've defeated zombies on a farm and saved my lady love from a contagion that would've turned her into one of the undead. I've slipped through the shadows as a masked vigilante, saving the innocent. I've even tunneled to the center of the earth in search of dinosaurs and defeated Nazi cultists.

And that's because for Todd, it's not about keeping his toys to himself. The thrill is in the collaboration, building the proverbial sandbox. He's told the tales of AEGIS through old time radio plays, gorgeous comic books, beautifully designed RPG manuals, gripping novels, and now, with a second anthology of short stories. In all of these endeavors, Todd has sought talented storytellers and artists to work alongside him in various capacities, making each entry into the AEGISverse a complex melding of experiences and points of view. For someone who had trouble finding herself in the genre, this has been a true delight to be a part of.

My hope as you delve once more into the mysterious, sometimes funny, and always fast-paced world of AEGIS Tales, is that no matter your background, race, gender identity or disability, that you will find yourself here, the hero of the story. That you will escape the world for a few hours and become the detective that befriends the Archduke of Hell, as in Rose Lamont's tale. Perhaps you'd prefer to be a soldier, come back from the dead with spectral powers as in one of Todd's stories. Or the wunderkind inventor of R.L. Pace's contributions. Maybe you'd prefer Colin Fisk's retired Valkyrie, Martin Shannon's waitress-turned powerful shaman, or Brina Williamson's lady race car driver and her sleuthy pals. Perhaps James Stubbs' undead gunslinger, back for another round, or Todd's dinosaur-hunting heroine in a lost world. Or maybe it's aliens for you, in which case you'll want to check out Paul J. Howard's tale of Martian technology and a rail-riding hobo.

Whatever your particular poison, I wish you well on your journey and remind you: avoid the stepping stones with moss on them, always keep your whip handy, never trust a monkey (no matter how cute), and drinking games are great for distracting silly men who think that you're just a pretty face.

Second Sight

by Todd Downing

Death does not discriminate. The first thing we learned when we deployed at the Western Front was that the Grim Reaper does not care one jot for a man's skin color—the only hue to which it shows any preference is the dark crimson pumping through his human veins, until the spark of life slips away and that precious red ceases forever.

The Army back home was still a segregated affair, and would be until after the war. So the makeup of the 369th Infantry was "colored", meaning mostly black soldiers with some Puerto Ricans (which we used to joke were there "for some spice"). We'd been given the nickname "The Black Rattlers" by The United States Army, and "Men of Bronze" by the French. The Germans called us "The Harlem Hellfighters", having firsthand experience with our ferocity on the field of battle. Because the

US Army wanted little to do with us in a combat capacity, we were loaned out to French command. Our uniforms were American olive drab khaki, but our helmets, rifles and kit were provided by the French.

My unit had already seen action at the Second Battle of the Marne, a shy month of hell. I lost track of my kills after twenty-seven. A particular night raid when we swept a German trench and captured four machine gun emplacements made it pointless to keep a tally of the individual dead. As a reward for our heroism in that campaign, we got sent to the front of the line in the Meuse-Argonne Offensive, and no man would return the same.

We went over the top just before noon on the 26th of September, following a six-hour French artillery barrage, which rendered the land, fortifications, people, and everything in our path the consistency of oatmeal. The first five miles of our advance was through pulverized barbed wire fortifications, where our main enemy was getting stuck in the sundered earth and getting cut on a random shard of metal. We encountered almost no resistance, save for the occasional surrendering prisoners, which we collected and sent back to our lines in small groups. As the sun crested and began its afternoon descent, however, we found the ease of the initial push had been deceptive.

Our objective was the town of Ripont, which lay just beyond a nearly impassible bog. Nonetheless, our spirits were high. Everyone knew the war was nearly over, perhaps especially the Germans. But that only gave them less to lose in the chaos of battle. As Captain Shaw waved us into the muddy bracken, I gripped the Berthier rifle in my calloused hands, checking the slide and making sure there was a round chambered and ready.

Although our French compatriots had shown us how to cut the tails from our wool overcoats so they wouldn't drag in the water and become weighted down, we were going to get far wetter and dirtier than our usual exposure in the trenches. Some of us opted to shed our coats before we entered, rolling them into our packs.

Two dozen men waded into the bog, bayonets fixed. "Slow going" doesn't even begin to describe the agonizing approach to the town. Step after herculean step, mere forward progress felt like wading through molasses. And then, as we came upon a copse of alder trees sprouting from a mound of mushy soil, the gates of hell opened and all the Devil's minions came out to play.

The dappled marshland was suddenly alive with the staccato beat of gunfire and wood splinters. Saplings and men alike were cut in half. Private Coverdale's head opened like a ripe coconut just to my right, spraying me with blood and viscera. Captain Shaw fell into the muck on my left, screaming at everyone to take cover. The Germans had left a machine gun crew as a rear guard to cover their retreat, supported by a sniper aloft in one of the larger trees. I fell to my belly behind a rotting log, trying to gauge where the fire was originating. I knew the wood was too soft to provide lasting cover—this would be a running fight. As much as one could "run" in knee-deep mud and brackish water.

"Desmond!" Captain Shaw shouted at me as bullets whizzed past, "Push forward to Jones' position and see if you can get eyes on that MG!" I glanced down and nodded at the bloodied point of an alder branch protruding from the bulk of his right calf, just above his puttee.

"Yessir!" I replied, nodding at the wound. "You better see to that, Captain."

Then, with a grunt and a splash, I was off. Clutching the Berthier tightly and keeping it above the muck and water, I staggered forward around the log and through the small grove of trees, most of which had been sheared off at about head-height. The sun was hanging red in the afternoon sky, casting long shadows from left to right across the bog. My leg bumped something that felt like a sand-bag. Glancing down, I saw a mud-covered hand with the college ring and knew it was Patterson. Half of him, anyway.

Another stream of bullets rocketed from just beyond the riverbank, between the swamp and the bombed-out town that was our battle objective. I hunched over to keep my head low, which made traveling through the mud that much harder. Twenty yards ahead and to the right stood a river boulder anchoring another copse of alder trees. Corporal Jones fired back from behind the big rock, sliding down to a squat to reload a three-round clip from his haversack. His stylish mustache was caked with mud already drying in the afternoon heat.

"Want some company?" I asked, peering through the gap between the rock and the larger of two main alder trunks sprouting from the wet ground.

"Wouldn't say no," Jones quipped, loading the metal clip with wet, trembling fingers.

"Captain wants eyes on the MG," I relayed. "Any thoughts on that?"

Jones nodded. "It's on the bank, just beyond that bunch of fallen trees, yonder." He tilted his head back in a general indicator of direction, and I noted the long wall of raw timber he was describing, about thirty yards away.

"What about the sniper?"

Jones shook his head. "That's another story," he frowned. "But I'm pretty sure he's placed somewhere west of here. Low sun is making it hard to pinpoint." He finished loading the rounds and snapped the bolt forward. "Goddamn Jerries gonna pay for Buzzy."

I glanced to Jones' left and realized Burt "Buzzy" Franklin lay face-down and mostly submerged in the water just north of the boulder. He'd gained the moniker from the clippered fade haircut he adopted on our arrival in France. He was a good soldier, a devil at dice, and a genuine laugh when morale was low. He'd be missed.

Another angry hail of bullets rocketed past our position, tearing through the brush and kicking up steaming splatters of mud. Behind the fallen trees, I could make out a small group of German soldiers trudging through the underbrush, one reaching toward his waist—readying a stick grenade.

Taking aim with my Berthier, I sighted right at his jawline and squeezed the trigger, feeling the comfortable recoil into my shoulder as the shot rang out. The lead soldier dropped out of sight in a mist of red, and moments later, amid panicked shouts, the swamp exploded with mud and body parts. A single boot splashed down to my left, jagged shard of leg bone sticking out the top. From my vantage behind the rock and looking upward, I saw a brief glimmer of light from a tall plane tree behind the soldier, right in front of the afternoon sun. It could have been a trick of the light or a spark of ignited fabric from the soldier's uniform, but it was an equally good bet the sniper was in that tree and the grenade blast had reflected off his scope.

I pulled the bolt back and slapped it forward. *Two shots left.* For a moment, I considered the F1 grenades I carried in my secondary haversack. I could lob one of the tiny gray pineapples like we used to chuck rocks at crows back on granddaddy's farm. But the tree itself was more than sixty yards distant. Even in my days as a college outfielder that would have been pushing it. No, the math didn't add up. I decided on a different tactic.

I took the blue steel Adrian helmet from my head, pulled a wet tree branch from the muck and inserted it, creating a dummy target. Slowly, I raised the helmet so that the crest just cleared the top left corner of our rock. A crack rang out from the woods and I felt the helmet jerk back and fall off the stick. But I wasn't watching that—my eyes were on the plane tree, about twenty feet up. The muzzle flash had come almost exactly from the location I'd seen the glint in the grenade explosion.

That was my target.

While Jones continued to pop shots at the MG crew, cursing under his breath at the Jerries, I took careful aim at the tree, held my breath, and squeezed the trigger. The Berthier barked, a cry rang out, and something heavy fell, catching in the lower branches.

I reached behind me into the water and grabbed my helmet, checking it over in my left hand. Sure enough, it now carried a tiny depression near the front crest, like a fingerprint in butter. The Adrian helmet was light, and never intended to deflect a direct bullet impact. It was specifically designed to minimize damage from grenade shrapnel and indirect fire. Pulling the strap back over my chin, I flagged Captain Shaw and waved the rest of the unit forward.

Another burst of machine gun fire tore through the wet brush, pulverizing the soggy wood and sending splinters flying every which way. I waited until the gun crew came to the end of the belt, when I would have three to five seconds while they reloaded.

I nudged Jones in the ribs, cocking the slide on my rifle. "Cover me," I said.

Like a well-choreographed dance, I dashed through the stagnant water and mud twenty yards to the wall of fallen trees, while Captain Shaw and the rest of our unit moved up to the rock by Corporal Jones. Now that the sniper was out of the game, I wouldn't have to worry about getting caught in a crossfire and hit from above. And the barking fire from ten more rifles at the rock would make an excellent distraction for what I wanted to do.

My new vantage behind the logs was far better to see the machine gun emplacement. It sat behind a ring of sandbags on the upward slope of a dusty hill about thirty yards to the northeast, the last obstacle between our unit and the village that was our objective. The Maxim gun had a crew of three: a gunner, a spotter and a loader. And it sounded like they were having problems with the reload. I could hear swearing and the clank of metal on metal. The gun had either overheated or jammed. Either way, I'd have to act fast.

Reaching into the bag, I grasped a grenade and pulled it free, extracting the pin with my teeth and releasing it in a high, overhand throw. It came down just short of the gun emplacement. The explosion did little but carve out a chunk of riverbank, shrapnel absorbed by the heavy sandbag barricade. I reached for a second grenade and threw with a bit more force, and this time the effort paid off. The metal pineapple came down right behind the machine gun, and the moment I heard it go off, I sprinted into action, slogging up the embankment like a knight and war horse in one. My lance was a long rifle tipped with two additional feet of bayonet, all force focused behind that sharp point. I saw spasms of motion behind the sandbags, and heard terrified cries and angry oaths, all in German. Within moments, I'd cleared the bog, sprinted up the embankment and leaped over the sandbags, landing with the full weight of my body behind the rifle. The German soldier looked up at me in shock, the bayonet protruding halfway from his ribcage. To his left, the machine gun's back end was chewed to pieces, the gun leaning nose-down over the barricade. The gunner's body lay flipped on its back, a mostly headless corpse. I turned my attention back to the soldier at the end of my pig-sticker and noticed the third crewman was already scampering up the hill toward the village.

Huffing and straining with the effort, I wrenched the rifle away from the soldier skewered on the end, to no avail. The bayonet had penetrated between the ribs and lodged in the spine. It wasn't coming out any time soon.

Almost without thinking, I reached down and pulled the dying soldier's sidearm from its holster, racking back the slide of the broom-handled Mauser and thumbing the safety off. Before I knew it, I'd popped a half-dozen shots into the retreating soldier's back. He collapsed and lay still in a heap.

Then I heard a voice yelling, "Forward!" and I realized it was mine. "MG is kaput! Let's go, boys!"

All was chaos as a rumbling, splashing herd of men came screaming through the marsh, swarming up the hill to where I stood, gasping for breath among the dead machine gun crew.

"Good work, private!" It was Shaw, limping up the hill with his leg bandaged as a small unit of my fellow Rattlers pushed up the last few yards to the outskirts of the village. "I'm putting you in for a commendation—you're a goddamn hero!"

I tossed the pistol aside, not having time to revel in the accomplishment, nor my captain's praise for the deed.

Suddenly a metallic pop erupted near the corner of an old farmhouse at the town's edge, someone yelled, "Gas!" and the men who'd advanced on the town scrambled to put on their filters.

"Mask on, Desmond," Shaw ordered, clapping me on the shoulder. "Let's go take us a town." Then he was gone, and I shrugged out of my pack to more easily access the canvas hood and filter we'd been issued, which hung from a cloth handle around my neck. I hated wearing the thing. It was dank and stuffy and smelled of piss—the common way for soldiers to seal the appliance. But better a whiff of pee than lungs full of phosgene or mustard gas. I struggled to get to hood on, and once properly situated, I realized I had no weapon. I picked up the stock of my rifle which was still stuck in the German soldier. Placing a boot on his chest for leverage, I heaved with all my strength, but his bones held the bayonet firmly and the release was bent. I quickly looked around for another weapon as Shaw ordered the advance on the town and the rest of my unit passed me on the hillside. A Mauser carbine lay on the ground just beyond the gun emplacement, but when I picked it up I found the slide was missing completely. Casting the rifle to the ground in disgust, I turned back to the Berthier and realized there was still one round loaded on the clip inside.

I hefted the stock once again, squeezing the trigger. There was a muffled shot and a spray of blood at point-blank range, and the corpse opened again. The blade retreated as the empty clip was ejected from the bottom of the rifle. It had been enough force to shatter the bones holding onto the bayonet. I quickly pressed another clip into the rifle and slapped the bolt forward, sprinting up the rise to rejoin my unit.

If the Germans knew the war was lost, they sure were acting otherwise. The village of Ripont was wrapped in a swath of what appeared to be mustard gas, like a sickly yellow fog bank creeping across the town square. But there was an additional layer of ghostly white mist just under the yellow, that would occasionally poke through as it undulated beneath. The town looked mostly deserted, except for the German troops occupying every second story with a window into the courtyard. This was going to be a bloodbath, one way or another.

Shaw patted my shoulder again as I approached. "There's our goddamn hero!"

A Chauchat crew arrived and set up at an angle to the first row of houses, opening fire in a straight line across the windows. Any dwellings that still had glass windows didn't after the machine gun tore through. The German rear guard now consisted of a few random infantry left in place as snipers, but the majority of them were put down in the first few salvos from our machine gun. But then the Chauchat locked up with a fatal jam—as they were famous for—and Captain Shaw waved us in. "Let's go, boys!"

Taking up position around the first corner of the farmhouse, I sent some covering fire into the second story of the bakery across the cobbled street as my fellow soldiers moved into the square. I counted down the ammo: *Three, two, one.* Each time I slid the bolt back, releasing the spent shell and racking a new round into place. One by one, enemy soldiers dropped where they stood or fell from the shattered window sills above. I moved from doorway to doorway, snapping off shots as they presented themselves. *Three, two, one.* Each time I chambered a third round, the empty clip ejected below and clattered to the stone street. Despite the knee-deep layer of toxic mist swirling around us, we were picking off the Jerries like low-hanging fruit. We had them on the run. Taking the town wasn't going to be a problem.

I reached into ammo bag and grabbed another clip, pushing it through the open slide as other men continued to fire around me. Despite the conditions, I felt absolutely safe, protected. Then I caught a split-second flash of light from an upper window across the square, and my head snapped back with the force of a bullet glancing off the left eyepiece of my gas mask. The hoods didn't have great visibility to begin with, but now there was a lateral crack across the lower third of the left lens, cutting my field of vision in half and making accuracy next to impossible. Turning back toward the shooter, angry and still in shock, I felt two sharp bursts of pain in my right side and shoulder. The rifle fell from my numb hands, clattering beneath the sea of chemical gas. I staggered back against the flower shop doorway, reaching toward the wounds out of instinct. Another shot rang out, and I felt my throat open at the collarbone.

"Jesus," I mumbled in bewilderment as I sank to my knees in the town square.

Another burst of pain from my left thigh, and a fourth in my abdomen, and darkness began to creep in around my cracked vision.

I fell forward onto my face, knocking the entire left lens free. My eyes seared, flushing wet, and I began to choke as I felt my lungs begin to burn.

Can't breathe.

And I died.

CR

My eyes fluttered open as I felt myself being supported aloft, gazing down over a stark scene. Two men wearing Rattlers uniforms gripped the handles of a stretched between them, carrying a soldier's body upon it. I couldn't make out the man in front, but the soldier holding up the back of the stretcher looked like Private Davies, a soft-spoken nineteen-year-old kid from Hell's Kitchen. We'd gone through Basic together. I tried to call out for him, but no sound came out, despite my exhaustive effort. Like a balloon tethered to the stretcher, I was tugged along with the two soldiers and their cargo, this dead Rattler in his tattered uniform, past the field hospital and toward a wagon stacked with corpses. I could only imagine the destination of the wagon.

As they approached the cart, setting the stretcher down ever so gently, a terrible truth washed over me—ice-cold like a Coney Island wave in the Spring. At that moment, I recognized the corpse on the stretcher.

He was me. And these two men were my burial detail.

I felt a strange recoil sensation, as if the invisible tether anchoring me above the man on the stretcher was plucked by an unseen hand. It was abrupt and filled my throat with bile. Suddenly I was pulled downward, and in an instant my lungs filled with air. I could tell I was on my back; the lumps through the canvas stretcher told me it was on the gravel road next to the field hospital. The dead man I'd seen below me was my actual body, and now I was back in it. Everything hurt like hell, and my lungs were on fire. I coughed, one of those earth-shaking coughs that you feel in your spine. Then I threw up everything I'd eaten since the previous night's dinner, and the residue of whatever chemical weapons had seeped into my system during the battle. I could barely manage to croak the word "help" between coughing and heaving my guts onto the road. The most frightening thing was that

I couldn't see. Everything was a murky, desolate void of color.

"Holy moley!" cried Davies. "He's alive!"

"Sweet Jesus!" shouted the other soldier, with an alarm that sounded like he'd seen a ghost at the foot of his bed. The quick footsteps of boots on gravel echoed in my ears. A sudden volley of shouted oaths and orders followed, and I felt the stretcher hoisted off the ground.

I must have passed out then, because the next thing I remembered was waking up with a splitting headache and still no vision. The place smelled of antiseptic soap and alcohol, and the troubled moans of wounded and dying men surrounded me on all sides. I knew I must be in the field hospital.

"Easy, soldier," said a soft voice from the dark. It was warm and feminine, and carried an emotional weight I couldn't begin to imagine. I felt a hand—presumably hers—on mine, turning my wrist to lay a cool finger across it, feeling my pulse. "You're safe now," she said.

I tried to make the words form in my throat, but only hoarse grunts emerged. "N-Nurse…" I sputtered.

"Don't try to talk," she instructed, releasing my arm and reaching up to arrange the pillow under my head. "I'm Dorothy, and you're in my care." She leaned over me, and I got the distinct scent of perfumed dusting powder through the sterile cleaning agents and disinfectants. I knew it was the only scent nurses were allowed to wear in the ward. "There's a bell on the table to your right," she said, placing my hand on the object as she described it. "If you need anything, ring it and I'll be right there."

I reached out instinctively, grasping her arm. With my left hand, I gestured at the bandages wrapped tightly around my eyes and skull. "Wh-What...happened?"

Expecting her to pull away at the sudden contact, I was pleasantly surprised to feel her other hand gently pat mine as I released her arm.

"You were wounded in the push through Ripont," she explained. "Took five slugs and full exposure to a cocktail of gas weapons."

I heard the stool creak as she stood, getting another whiff of dusting powder as she bent, checking my bandages.

"Private Desmond," she said, an almost bewildered note to her voice, "you're very lucky to be alive."

"Th-Thank you," I hissed from my throat.

She patted my arm and stood over the bed. Somehow I knew she was smiling. "Just rest," she said wistfully. "Rest and heal."

Though I didn't know it at the time, the tinge of sadness in her voice was due to the knowledge that I'd never see again. At least, not how normal people see.

CR

"Let's see how those peepers are getting on, shall we?"

The doctor's voice was pleasant, smooth as a vintage single-malt scotch. His accent was Mid-Atlantic, the type we'd start hearing on the radio in just a few short years. He was an American colonel, I'd gathered, by the name of Starr, and he always stopped by my bedside for a quick chat while on his morning rounds. Eventually I was able to make more coherent conversation than the hissing croaks the gas had initially reduced me to, and we were able to talk about where we grew up and how surprisingly alike our families were.

I'd spent two weeks in this hospital, literally in the dark, as the dulcet-toned Colonel Starr tended to his patients. Most of us were either French, or Americans under French command, like the Rattlers—who were now becoming better-known by their German nickname: The Harlem Hellfighters. By now, I'd mapped out the entire ward, including the hallways, the WC, and the garden outside the former church that had been converted for its current medical purpose. I'd also formed an impression of every patient, doctor, nurse and orderly in the place, especially nurse Dorothy Brown. Now it was time for the doctor to trim away the bandages from around my eyes and see what was what.

The pressure at my temples, what had been an endless, dull ache, was relieved as the colonel cut away the rolls of gauze around my head and eyes. I could feel layers come away, and yet saw no intrusion of sunlight. Everything was still as dark as it had been for the past two weeks. Finally, I felt the last of the gauze fall away, and the colonel's fingers pry the twin cotton pads from my orbital sockets. I blinked once, twice—nothing but darkness. My thoughts returned to Sunday school, and I remembered a passage from Genesis: *And the earth was without form, and void; and darkness was upon the face of the deep.*

"What do you see, Private Desmond?" Colonel Starr inquired, his hands gently changing the position of my head as he observed the extent of my damage.

"Nothing," I replied, husky and heavy from deep in my chest. "Not a damn thing."

"Not surprising, really. The damage to the corneas and the optic nerves was extensive."

Something halted in his breath. I could tell he wasn't satisfied. Neither was I, of course. The fact that I wouldn't be the only blind veteran of this war was cold comfort.

Colonel Starr cleared his throat. "There's a specialist in Paris," he began. "I think we'll try to get you in there—"

And at precisely that moment, the lights came on. All of them, all at once. It was as if the noonday sun had dropped right into the ward, white-hot and blinding. Except I was already blind, and this light was searing away the darkness. Every nerve ending in my skull screamed in agony, and I threw my arms across my eyes to stop the pain, stop the light seeping through, to no avail. The pitiful cries of a wounded soldier surrounded my bed, and I realized they were coming from my own throat. I felt hands on my shoulders, both the colonel's and Nurse Brown's. They gently tried to steady me as I rocked back and forth in my bed, unable to escape the light. *Let there be light*, indeed.

After what seemed like an eternity, but was likely not more than several seconds, the pain receded, and my arms dropped away from my face. My eyes fluttered open, and the light retreated to a normal level in flashes, like shells bursting in a night barrage across No Man's Land. I could see shapes now; shadows and highlights and nuance. It was all a blurry landscape, but there was depth and form. My ravaged eyes welled with tears, and I blinked, washing them with my natural saline. It stung like nettles, or getting lemon juice in a cut. But I let it sting, breathing deeply with damaged lungs as those hands held me.

"How we doing, Desmond?" the colonel asked. "You want something for the pain?"

My head shook no without my conscious input. Apparently I needed clarity for what was to come. "No," I explained. "I'm okay."

The doctor gave some instructions to Nurse Brown, who took a seat beside my bed and continued to monitor my condition. Colonel Starr then disappeared on his regular rounds, promising to return later in the afternoon. I sat up in bed, blinking those lemon juice tears, washing my eyes in stinging agony. After a good twenty minutes, the pain dulled and my vision became clearer and deeper. Shapes, both near and far, were clearly defined. What's more, every shape seemed to radiate with a sort of prism of light. I'd learn later that "halo effects" are common among victims of optical injuries. I'd also come to understand that what I was seeing wasn't a simple halo effect. I glanced to my right, looking into the face of Nurse Dorothy Brown, one of several kind and compassionate medics who had cared for me these past two weeks, but by far my favorite of the bunch. Her face was not more than three feet from mine, and yet gazing at her felt like looking at an unfinished portrait. As much as I'd discovered basic depth and detail in my surroundings, finer features were still a jigsaw puzzle. However, those prismatic rays of light emanated more brightly from her than from the other inanimate objects I'd focused on.

As I glanced around the ward, I noticed every bed had a soldier in it, and every soldier radiated a bright aura of light—like the corona of an eclipse, flickering and flaring in a brilliant dance. Then something in the hallway caught my attention. A soldier seemed to be walking across the hall, but there was no form to his body. The light aura still radiated, but it flared around the outside as if from an invisible silhouette. There was no solid substance to him. Thinking it just another manifestation of my injury, I initially paid it no heed.

For another week, I kept absorbing my surroundings, my vision becoming clearer and more detailed. Colonel Starr's opinion was that everything I was "seeing" was an optical illusion caused by my injured optic nerves sending ghost images to my brain. He couldn't explain how I was able to navigate the ward, the hospital and the grounds, as if I could see perfectly. One theory was that I'd spent enough time effectively "blind" that I'd formed a sort of three-dimensional map of my environment based on my heightened hearing and smell. But when we left the hospital to see his specialist in Paris, and I was still in command of my surroundings, he was officially out of ideas.

It was Friday, the 1st of November. I recall the day was brisk and clear following a week of rain. News was the Central Powers were beaten. The Jerries were on the run, and an armistice was close at hand. A large influx of wounded soldiers had come through the hospital in recent weeks, testament to the final push along the Western Front. French grenadiers, American marines, and even some British Gurkha shock troops from Nepal. Even as I got better discerning faces and details, I never lost the sensation of the "ghost halos". At all hours of the day or night, they'd wander the hallways among the wards. Often, when a soldier died in his bed, I could watch as a "ghost halo" stood from the bed in which the soldier lay, wandering away into the hall or out into the garden. I didn't speak of it to Colonel Starr. When Dorothy came to get me ready for transport, I was already dressed.

"I see someone's excited to get to Paris," she smiled, brilliant shards of light dancing across her head and shoulders.

"Can't wait to see it," I joked.

When we exited the hospital, I found the colonel had requisitioned a staff car for the trip, instead of an ambulance. Nurse Brown and I sat in the backseat, while a young British corporal drove. As we passed along gravel roads, muddy country lanes and hedgerows, we passed columns of the refugees and dispossessed: those made homeless from the ravages of Total War. They were often in the company of Allied soldiers, marching hundreds of German and Austrian prisoners to camps southwest of the Hindenburg Line. I saw the same sparkles of light emanate from every living person, and hundreds more of the phantom halos in their midst.

Paris was alive with high spirits and the same auras of light, and so many phantoms I could not hazard an accurate number. Soldiers home from the front hobbled around on crutches, taxis honked and rattled through the streets, and Parisian ladies laden with parcels wore bright smiles with their Fall fashions.

The visit to the specialist went much as I expected. Read these letters, look into this light, follow my finger. The elderly French ophthalmologist with a well-trimmed beard and crisp, white smock could not determine why I was clearly able to see when all external conditions would indicate I should not. Much to my surprise, Nurse Brown didn't leave it at that. The German gas weapons had affected me—altered me somehow—giving me not only normal sight, but sight beyond. A *second sight*, she said. Instinct told me she was right.

We stayed the night in Paris, and after that, I knew I would not be going home to New York.

I awoke at 0200 to the sight of two phantom auras in my hotel room. No discernible features, only the absence thereof, radiating a red-tinted halo from a blank outline. Whatever these things were, I knew in my gut they weren't human, and they meant me harm. Without thinking, I leaped from the bed, and found myself hurtling toward the intruders. Whereas most people must obey the laws of physics and land when they jump, I did not fall—I rocketed forward fists balled into hammers of rage and sheer willpower. Each fist penetrated a silhouette, hands icy on contact. A static discharge as my energy channeled through each of my hands, a brief shriek of agony from either side, and it was over.

I opened my eyes, facing the inside of my hotel room door. Glancing down, I noticed my feet hovered about ten inches off the floor. My hands glowed white and purple, crackling with shards of pure light. Turning to look over my shoulder, I saw my sleeping form still tucked cozily in bed, breathing steadily. I watched the rhythmic inhalation and exhalation for a minute, satisfied that my body would be safe for the time being. Then, turning back to the door, I willed myself forward, and sailed through it.

The hotel corridor I was expecting to be empty was full of phantom halos. They were everywhere. But these specters wandered without apparent purpose, and cleared out of my way as I floated past them. The hallway terminated at a window made of rectangular panes, which I passed through as easily as a draft of air. Knowing I was not in a corporeal body had rid me of any fear of falling or injury, and I sailed gently to the street below, merely focusing my will to make it happen.

A hack drawn by a single horse was pulling away from the curb, and my sudden descent from above sent the poor animal into a panic. Shrieking, it reared and strained at its harness, causing the cabbie to curse and fight with the reins. I gently sailed forward and reached out, making contact with the horse, stroking its neck softly, sending calm intent through my hand. Immediately, the beast settled, and I ascended away as the cabbie came down to check on it. Like a human kite, I sailed over the City of Lights, smelling the myriad scents of food, people, animals, and industry.

I descended into the *Jardin des Tuileries*, near a slumbering man on a bench. He wore a heavy wool French Army coat, and though his left thigh was tucked under him, I could tell his leg had been amputated below the knee. His aura danced with the same sparks of light that I saw on most living beings, only dimmer and less distinct. I could sense the man's despair, and his morphine addiction, as easily as smelling fresh bread from the oven. By instinct, I reached out, focusing my will through my arms. A crackle of energy buzzed through both of us as I made contact, pushing the sadness away, purging the horror and helplessness—casting light into the dark. The man's body began to shake and tremble, and a trickle of foamy bile spewed from the corner of his mouth. After a few brief, uncomfortable moments, he settled into a deep sleep, breathing normally. The aura around his body surged with new radiance. I was confident that whatever challenges that veteran faced in the future, addiction and shell-shock wouldn't be among them.

My head began to swim, and I knew I'd pushed myself too far in a small amount of time. A few phantom halos in the vicinity began to focus on my location, perhaps sensing weakness. I glanced down at the soldier again, and when I looked up, the phantoms had multiplied. Looking left and right, I could see them springing up from the ground, almost generating out of nowhere before my eyes. Before I knew what was happening, I was surrounded by a horde of faceless phantoms, crowding in from all sides, hungry for the energy I was giving off. For the first time since my apparent death on the cobbled street of Ripont, I felt genuine terror. Terror of my psychic form being torn apart and consumed by these ravenous beings. I realized this fear was keeping my feet anchored to the ground, and that the phantoms must sense fear as weakness. It was weakness that attracted them, much like blood in the water attracts a shark. I had to refocus my will, dig deep within my very soul and produce the strength that would keep the ghosts at bay. One featureless hand reached out and touched my shoulder, and an icy chill struck at my heart. For a moment, I was lost in panic. Oblivion scratched at the door.

But then something remarkable happened.

"Easy, soldier," said a soft voice from the dark.

Clamping my eyes shut, I recalled the dark, featureless landscape of my bandaged vision. I remembered the relative peace and quiet of the hospital ward, and the gentle, soothing hand of Nurse Brown. A sensation of renewed vigor filled the well of my spirit, and I felt my feet leave the ground. I lifted into the air and soared above Paris with eyes still closed, letting the mental picture of my hotel room guide me back to safety.

I found my body still sleeping peacefully in the hotel room. A simple thought was all it took to reunite my astral form with the corporeal one. For the first time since arriving at the front, I didn't dream of artillery barrages or gas attacks. Just quiet stillness.

CR

I awoke feeling better than I ever had, and made the decision to tell Nurse Brown about my experience over breakfast. After her initial shock wore off, I demonstrated the finer points of astral travel and energy manipulation in the hotel lounge. It was then I discovered I could project my astral form to become visible through the same force of will I employed to soar through the sky, heal a veteran's psychic afflictions, or destroy a phantom intent on evil. Over time, I discovered I could use most of these abilities while still conscious, in my corporeal body. Astonished, Dorothy promised we'd keep in contact after the war. Colonel Starr would likely have some new theories. In the meantime, she and Starr were due to head back to New York, engaged to be married. I jokingly asked what the rush was, fully able to tell from the light emanating from her that she was pregnant.

As expected, the Armistice happened a week and a half later. Like more than a few black American soldiers, I opted to remain in France after being discharged. I began to work with the French government, helping veterans reintegrate to the workforce, helping American military expats like me start a new life "Over There". After months of growing out a curly beard, I started to shave again. I rented a spa-cious loft in an old building on *Rue Chaudron*, across the tracks from the cemetery, where I could paint on days when I wasn't doing my government work, and which made a nice base of operations for my nighttime activities. I cut up some motorcycle leathers and found a hooded cloak among the offerings at a theater costume sale. Sometimes I went out in my body, and sometimes I left it at home. I got good enough, precise enough, to be able to knock a thief's astral body out of its corporeal counterpart long enough to allow his victim to get away. When the newspapers began reporting a series of crimes thwarted by a ghostly figure in black, I knew I was on the right path.

Sometime in April 1922, I received a telegram from Colonel Starr, and he came up to the loft to chat. He was working with this consortium of American industrialists, developing a network of adventurers and "gifted" folks like me, to face down a megalomaniac bent on world domination through arcane means. At first, I told him I'd had my fill of tyrants trying to take over the world, but the more I thought about it, the more sense it made that I would use the powerful gift given to me—at one hell of a cost—for the greater good of humanity. Starr left a calling card with the name Colonel Stephen Shaw on it, told me I'd be hearing from him. Apparently Shaw was a higher-up at MI-6 in London, and was putting together a group of gifted people irrevocably changed by the war to help keep the delicate peace in Europe.

By the time Shaw caught up to me, it was May. He arrived at the door to my loft in a trench coat, a wrapped bottle of whiskey under one arm, a valise under the other. He was the archetypal suave English gentleman, with pomade in his prematurely white hair and a patch over his left eye. The man didn't waste time: he had some individual candidates, but needed someone to actually lead the squad the was forming.

"You were awarded a Distinguished Service medal and the *Croix de guerre,*" Shaw rattled off in his posh English accent. "And you led your squad across a nearly impenetrable swamp, single-handedly taking out a sniper and a three-man machine gun emplacement. Ripont was taken due to your efforts."

"Just doing what had to be done, Colonel." I could read from his aura's hue that his intent was good. "Who else have you got?"

He opened his leather valise and tossed a stack of file folders on my dining table. "A French vampire, an English robot, and a disfigured Gurkha who fights like a demon."

"Sounds like a motley crew," I remarked, without a hint of irony.

"Some might think it a bit...weird," Shaw replied.

I smirked as I flipped open the first folder. "Colonel," I said, "the moment I stepped off the boat in France, my life's been nothing *but* weird." As I read over the dossiers, I could tell this bunch would need some coaching, some guidance to whip them into shape as an effective force for good. "What are we calling this unit?"

Shaw pulled up a chair and fished a cigarette from the pack in his inside breast pocket. "We've been working with *The Altered*."

The Altered, I thought. *Seems appropriate.*

"Colonel, with a name like that, how could The Seer refuse?"

Operation Icarus

by R.L. Pace

August 1926

Felix Fogarty had become something of a celebrity among AEGIS forces since the Shanghai incident. Escaping his nearly deadly encounter with Song Li and the Black Dog alone might have earned him that status given their sinister association with the *Astrum Argentum*, but managing to simultaneously seize the secret plans and destroy the prototype anti-gravity machine—while burning down a sizable portion of the waterfront—had secured borderline legendary status. And the weeks-long journey to Edison's workshop in West Orange, New Jersey hadn't been wasted either.

Comfortably ensconced in a first class cabin aboard the *RMS Empress of Asia*, Felix had spent the voyage under the watchful eye of bodyguards thoughtfully provided by Joe

Frankels, his section chief in China. At six-three with a disheveled shock of coppery hair blending in with the other passengers for the two week crossing carried a low hope of success. Plus, the need for a large table and complete privacy-secrecy even-mandated the extra space and the room service too.

Armed with sheaves of drafting paper, a host of T-squares, triangles, French curves, rulers and writing instruments, he was painstakingly recreating—from his photographic memory—the blueprints he had been sent to collect from the Club Lusitano, which is where the conflagration that sped through a swath of Shanghai began. The pier fire that consumed the yacht club had only burnished his newfound fame.

When the ship docked in Vancouver, British Columbia at the Canadian Pacific Steamship pier and her four steam turbine props had gone still Felix was greeted at the pier with a new phalanx of AEGIS guardians and hustled off for a rendezvous with airship *Hephaestus* for the final legs. Because it was a repair, recovery and salvage vessel the ship bristled with defensive weapons. Slow, with cramped crew quarters but a huge cargo and maintenance bay, it wasn't a glamorous ride but it was nearly impregnable when airborne.

No one was taking any chances with Felix, his brain or the newly recreated blueprints.

☙

June 1927

"It helps if you think of electrical circuits like plumbing. Wires are the pipes, electricity the water and the various other parts like tubes, resistors, condensers and rectifiers are basically valves that alter where, how, and how much the current flows." Felix was trying to explain where the vast sums of money being spent on his development project were going. Edison was congenial as host; Henry Ford was off wandering around the rest of the massive shop inspecting things Fogarty was pretty certain he knew little about. It was Harvey Firestone who had been peppering him with questions for the better part of an hour.

"Most expensive toilet we've ever plumbed!" Firestone groused, not entirely in jest.

"Well Harvey," Edison broke in, "Plumbing is already invented. We're starting almost from scratch here."

"Do you think Silver Star is going to wait around while you try to invent another light bulb?"

Edison laughed. "Probably not, but if not for Wonder Man here, they would surely be far more dangerous than they already are."

From across the shop a startled cry rang out as a technician drifted toward the ceiling bathed in an eerie blue glow and an equally startled Henry Ford quickly flipped down the switch he had tentatively activated. The light disappeared and the technician fell five feet to the floor. Chagrined, Ford mumbled an apology and hurried back to the group. The technician was left rubbing his hip, anticipating quite a bruise the following day.

"I see you found our main effort," Edison said as the auto magnate rejoined the men. "We call it 'Project Icarus'."

"I don't doubt it, but what use is it? Does it just throw stuff in the air?"

"For now, yes, that's about it. But figuring out what to use it for is what we are doing." Edison the entrepreneur was getting enthusiastic. "Imagine elevators with the compartment and the brakes as the only moving part! Or trains that glide above the tracks. No more clickety-clack droning in your ears." He eyed Ford with a mischievous grin, "or automobiles with no engines or wheels."

"Don't let Rockefeller hear that. He'll buy all three of us and put us afloat in the Atlantic."

"The main problem, gentlemen," Fogarty interrupted, "is portability. How do we make it small enough to be useful and how do we throttle the lift? It's not just a rhetorical question, and that is where most of the money is being used."

"And do you have any progress to report on that front?" Firestone clearly wanted to get down to brass tacks.

"Well, yes and no. Some of the biggest issues with electrical circuits, besides the physical volume they occupy, are power consumption, heat and fragility. Tubes just aren't very efficient. In a nutshell we have to reduce the size of the plumbing from oil pipeline scale to drinking fountain size. But we have made a few discoveries that may help. If you'll follow me..."

Suddenly an arc from a high voltage transformer lit up the shop with a brilliant flash. Turning toward the source the Vagabonds were transfixed as a worker apparently tidying up a workbench shorted a circuit with his own body and was held in a rigor tension as the voltage coursed through him. Felix sprinted toward the man, grabbing a wooden hook-pole as he went. He jammed the hook into a massive knife switch eye pulling it open. The worker collapsed to the floor, and before anyone could reach him to render aid he began dissolving into a thick mass of smoke.

Fogarty had seen this before in Shanghai and began shouting commands. "Hit the button, Ed. We've been infiltrated!" He raced back to the trio of industrialists, their mouths agape in horror, as a klaxon blared and doors began swinging shut. "C'mon, we have get you to a safe place right now!"

Herding the group toward the far end of the cavern-like facility, Felix could see AEGIS ground forces already pouring onto the grounds and into the building. Hustling his charges along, he grunted with effort to swing open a heavy steel door leading to a set of stairs which descended into a basement. There they were met by four armed security men. "Get these men to the Oar Lock and seal it off. No one but me or Chief Esterhaus releases you. Got that?"

"Yessir, Felix. Do you have an estimate?"

"Complete assessment and interrogation. Could be several hours. No one in or out."

"Gentlemen," the guard intoned seriously, "please follow me. Your cooperation is required."

Firestone began to object but Edison put a hand on his shoulder and shook his head. "Let them do their work, Harvey. We'll be safe."

Now that his civilian charges had been handed off Fogarty could concentrate on the issue at hand. He pulled the Iver-Johnson Model Three .38 revolver from his jacket pocket, flipped open the cylinder to check his ammo, then closed it with grim resolve. AEGIS troops seemed to have secured the shop so he headed to inspect what remained of the Silver Star agent. He knew it wouldn't be much, but any clue would help.

"What do you think, Eula? How did we end up with a Silver Star janitor?"

All five feet of Security Chief Eula Esterhaus craned her neck to make eye contact with Fogarty. "Too early to tell. But all daytime staff and personnel are accounted for and under wraps in the mess hall." She holstered her Colt .45 automatic, standard sidearm issue for officers of AEGIS security. The weapon looked like a cannon in her small hands but Felix knew her aim was deadly as she had demonstrated on the training range many times and, he suspected, in the field as well.

"My agents are collecting overnight staff to bring them in too. Family background checks are already under way to see if we missed anything when we hired new people." At twenty nine years of age she was blessed with a flawless deep olive skin to go with a tidy bob of chestnut hair and matching eye color. Her trim figure looked ready to handle bad guys of any heft or threat. An early AEGIS hire, Eula Esterhaus had worked undercover in the Mediterranean for the first few years, before taking command of the brand new Security division at headquarters. She was smart, capable and seemed embarrassed that this breach had happened on her watch.

"Don't let it bother you," Felix said as he noted nearby agents. "This is a big operation, and so is *Astrum Argentum*. Crowley has eyes and ears nearly everywhere. Little wonder he managed to put someone inside our home turf." Fogarty sat in an oak office chair so he could be eye to eye. "Who's doing interrogation?"

"Don Jackson and Emily Louis. Tag team. What bothers me is I've seen dozens of his minions go up in sparkly smoke and we're still no closer to a method to identify them beforehand. It's my home turf and it makes me mad."

"Well, let's get to work." Felix was all business but like his Security Chief, this identification problem bothered him too.

◌◌

"Damn the luck! Damn! Damn! Damn! Stupid mistakes, over and over again! This has got to stop." Song Li was a lithe Asian tiger on the prowl, and despite her petite physical status, men more than twice her size averted their eyes or cowered fearfully at her seething rage. The debacle in Shanghai hung over her reputation like a sword of Damocles; threatening to slice her head off at the neck if she failed Aleister Crowley again. How the Black Dog had avoided repercussions was beyond her, and the fact he actually got a promotion was particularly galling. Now, from her new headquarters in Paterson, New Jersey—chosen for its proximity to Edison's workshop—she was again thwarted: this time by just plain bad luck. It had taken months to recruit a suitable candidate and yet more time to finally get him in place. All that work was gone in a literal puff of smoke. Worse, AEGIS was alerted to their own vulnerability and the obvious presence of *Astrum Argentum* agents.

Their security would tighten even more and the pace of the research would quicken.

As she pondered her situation Song Li realized that failure might be a blessing in disguise. Let them do the work then take it from them. Crowley, notoriously impatient, could be dealt with if a bigger payoff seemed likely. It would have to do.

"We need a new plan," she mumbled to herself. Then loudly to the occupants of the dimly-lit meeting room, "What are you standing around for? Don't you have something to do? Get out of here, I need to think." Pulling out a drawer in her desk she retrieved a glass, withdrew a bottle of Jack Daniel's Tennessee Sour Mash Whiskey and poured two fingers. Downing it in a single gulp she poured another, leaned back in her chair and closed her eyes.

ॐ

February 1928

It had been an autumn and winter of hard work and significant change. New security measures were put in place, new plans laid and an accelerated research effort made. Felix Fogarty had been sent by AEGIS Command to

Seattle in the Pacific Northwest, presumably for specialized training in field airship operations, then spent a month with Nikola Tesla. It was his considered opinion that Tesla was the better theoretician, Edison the better practical uses man. Since Tesla couldn't stand Edison —and the reverse could be said if Edison actually remembered the man—Felix tried to be circumspect when he felt it was necessary to theorize wildly with someone smarter than he was. Tesla really understood the imagination end of inventing.

Eula Esterhaus had been promoted. She was leading AEGIS special covert operations worldwide, which meant she was flitting around the planet in an airship outfitted especially for her needs. It sported exotic new equipment, greater lift capacity, was faster with a smaller overall envelope than the larger Daedalus class ships. If everything checked out *Athena* just might become the flagship of a new class.

Shanghai Bureau Chief Joe Frankels had also moved up, taking over the role of Security Chief. His no nonsense approach and extensive field experience was useful, but it was his relationship with Fogarty that made it easy for Edison to accept the replacement recommendation of his exiting security officer.

Felix, with his outsized talent in languages plus practical theory in electrical circuits and mechanical design was now set to become a lynch pin of the West Orange research department and the perfect man to liaise with facilities around the world. About half of Frankel's new job was keeping this Wonder Man safe.

CR

Fogarty clambered out of a Model A Ford followed by five burly men onto the snow covered streets of West Orange. The winter landscape had a sepia tone quality in shades of gray washed in pale amber in the twilight. They were returning from a skiing expedition to Mt. Mansfield in Vermont, which had consisted mostly of trudging through snowdrifts and periodically manhandling the car back onto the road. There were even a few minutes of ski time to be had. To a man they were exhausted and glad to be back at headquarters. Guarding the wunderkind was hard work.

For his part the subject of all this protection made his way to Frankels security office, where he dumped his bag and collapsed onto a chesterfield sofa. Joe glanced up briefly then returned to the report he was editing.

"So," Frankels began, "mission accomplished?"

"I think so, Joe. I've been as visible as I could be for most of the winter. Do you think they are paying attention?"

"Count on it, son. I have reliable information in that regard. They are definitely watching."

"So on to the next thing then, I guess."

"Yep, time to convene a meeting of the Vagabonds." Frankels looked up and ran his right hand over his bald pate. ""They're gathering at Harbel Manor, and expecting you tomorrow."

"Then it's the overnight train to see the Rubber King." With that Felix scooped up his haversack and was out the door.

ℭ

"He's on the move again—heading for Akron." Song Li was talking to Aleister Crowley telephonically via the transatlantic cable activated less than two years earlier. "I think this is when we make our move."

"I've been more than patient up till now, Major. Waiting for AEGIS to perfect this technology was a risk worth taking, but only if your plan succeeds. If not, well...the consequences might be catastrophic. I hope, for your sake, they aren't."

The ominous tone left her shaken as she hung up the earpiece. It was time to set events in motion. Time to avenge herself of Felix Fogarty.

CR

Aboard the night train

Felix, carrying two leather blueprint cases, and his cadre of guards made their way to Hoboken Station where they boarded a train bound for Akron. One guard settled in with Fogarty in one compartment and two men each occupied the adjacent spaces.

Song Li was in *mufti*, having shed the distinctive black uniform of the Silver Star in favor of the pajama-like clothes and quilted jacket of a Chinese peasant. She had braided her hair to resemble the Qing Dynasty *queue* mostly worn by men and with a round skull cap covering the rest of her head. Sitting two cars forward, she watched her nemesis as he boarded. With a nod, a dozen other members of the Order paired off and moved to other coaches, waiting for the train to get underway.

Each man had his orders: recover the blueprints, kill Fogarty and all the other AEGIS operatives. She consulted her Ball Railroad Chronometer pocket watch. Less than two hours, she thought. He had escaped alive once before to her regret. She wouldn't make the same mistake twice.

Once underway the train finally cleared the metropolitan area and settled into a rhythm of rail song punctuated with the occasion staccato of crossing points as it rolled westward through Allentown, Hershey, and toward Harrisburg. Dark, rural landscapes occasionally illuminated by a streetlight in some hamlet, slipped by as they headed west and then eventually to their destination.

In Harrisburg they stopped to take on coal and water and several passengers disembarked to stretch their legs or buy a hot dog from a vendor hoping for a late evening sale. A few new passengers boarded when the conductor called all aboard and once again the train got underway.

CR

West Orange

Precisely on schedule, a Captain of the Silver Star dropped his hand and more than a hundred troops stormed the laboratory, workshop and home of Thomas Edison, almost completely overrunning AEGIS Headquarters, spreading destruction wherever they went and death whenever they could. Joe Frankels was routed from his office with a flurry of automatic weapons fire. He fell while streaking across the garden and lay still, face down in the snow covered grass. It was over in moments. Components were swiftly disassembled by Silver Star technicians and spirited away, the fallen AEGIS agents left where they dropped. It took less than fifteen minutes and when they were gone little of technical value remained behind.

CR

Aboard the night train

Felix was bored. He had completed two crosswords and eaten the three hot dogs his traveling companion returned with, getting mustard on his tie, much to his annoyance. Rising, he stuck his head into the companionway and, seeing nothing in either direction, sighed deeply and sat back down.

"Why don't you get some shuteye, Ed. Looks like a quiet night."

"Yeah, but no thanks. Better you should do. Busy times coming."

"Not the least bit sleepy. Maybe I'll look at the blueprints again." He opened one of the cases pulling out a couple of sheets of plans. Spreading one across his knees he began tracing a line with his finger. There was a tap on the compartment door.

"Tickets, please." A conductor held his ticket punch in his left hand.

Ed started to reach into his jacket while Fogarty set the plans to one side but the conductor swung a pistol with his right hand and fired two shots point blank into Ed's chest. Felix kicked at the gun, leaped to his feet and delivered a powerful blow to the man's solar plexus, shoving him into the companionway. He jumped back as gunfire erupted from both ends of the car.

Slapping off the light switch, he grabbed the cases and began climbing out the window to escape to the roof of the car. His long arms easily reached the walkway frame and he hoisted himself upward, barely clearing the compartment as Song Li stepped over the inert form of the bodyguard.

"Get him," she screamed to her henchmen clogging the doorway. "He's on the roof. And get the plans. Don't wait for me!"

The train hadn't yet reached full speed and was barely past the outskirts of town. Fogarty dashed across the car arriving at the front just as a Silver Star operative poked his head up for a look. Not even slowing down, he delivered a solid size-twelve right to the bridge of his nose, sending him to his death and smoky dissolution beneath the train. Smudge and grit belched from the locomotive stack as he moved forward. Song Li had gained the rooftop as well and with her flashlight and MP18 machine gun trained on her quarry she yelled out, "Give it up, Fogarty. You've got no help. All five of your men are dead and I have ten more men with me. Hand over the blueprints and I'll let you go: For old time's sake." She had no intention of honoring that promise.

"I find your offer generous and, forgive me, unbelievable. *Wo ningyuan xian si.*"

"So you speak Mandarin? Very talented. You'd rather die first? *Nizi bian.* Suit yourself."

As her finger closed on the trigger the train lurched as it slowed to make the turn to cross the Susquehanna River on the Rockville Bridge. Felix fell forward, losing his grip on the cases. Song Li's shot went wide but the blueprints slid off the car onto the tracks below. Immediately three Silver Star agents tumbled after them, their glow lamps at full power racing back to recover the containers. Song Li sent a triumphant smile Fogarty's way as he regained his footing. The air warmed slightly as the effect from the river arose to engulf the train.

"I win this time. You lose." She pulled the trigger, bullets barked from the barrel and the wonder man Felix Fogarty tumbled off the train and into the embrace of the river below.

CR

March 1928

Among his rank and file followers Aleister Crowley's home in the bucolic English countryside was simply know as Chateau Crow. Unless invited, or commanded, no one dropped in to this estate. Despite its impressive exterior demeanor, inside, the owner's obsession with the occult, off-world technology and the paranormal was manifest. It was from his collection of objects and artifacts he drew not only inspiration, but considerable personal power as well.

Major Li had been commanded to appear for an audience and she waited nervously to be summoned in one of what she imagined must be a dozen antechambers. She checked her uniform tunic and adjusted her cap emblazoned with the star emblem of Crowley's *Astrum Argentum* forces. An aide consulted a clock near the door and nodded. Taking a hard swallow, Li walked into the next room.

"Major Li, welcome to my home. Congratulations on the success of your recent mission. I believe it will be a great boon to my efforts." His smile was less than reassuring.

"Thank you, sir. It was just as we planned, with a minimum of losses."

"Yes, quite. Four dead. A trifling relative to our other encounters with AEGIS and easily replaced."

"Is there news regarding the project?"

"Mm, yes. The blueprints are quite thorough. Our chief scientist was very enthusiastic, but did warn it would take at least two years to build the new device. That actually puts us ahead of the project timeline before the unpleasantness in Shanghai. Very fortuitous, and a clever idea. Which brings me to you."

"Yes sir?" Her skin crawled with fear and a misty sheen of sweat broke out on her upper lip.

"Your involvement in this project is complete. You'll be needing a new assignment. And that will require your promotion to Colonel. Come, let's take a look at the dossier for your expedition to *Isla de Muerte Silenciosa*. It's a small place, really. Just a dot on the globe, but rumor has it the Golden Panther of the Incas is hidden somewhere there. Your mission is to find it and return it here to me. Maria Blutig will transport you and your command to South America where you will create a base of operations in Ecuador in the charming, if poverty-stricken coastal village of Esmeraldas. You have earned some time off. Use it wisely and report for embarkation Monday April second at our aerodrome in Farnsworth."

"Thank you, sir. By the way what does the name mean?"

"The Island of Silent Death."

"I see. Well, again thank you. I won't disappoint you, sir."

"I've no doubt about that," he replied dryly. "I'm sure you wouldn't want to risk such an outcome."

CR

April 1928

The campsite was a gorgeous meadow alive with bees buzzing industriously among the early wildflowers nestled in a nearly inaccessible valley in the Adirondack mountains. Sitting around the campfire were the members of the Vagabonds. Henry Ford and Harvey Firestone were devotees of camping, which is how their group nickname came about. Edison enjoyed it as well, when done in the style to which they were accustomed, which included staff, an entourage of vehicles carrying linens, china, silver, four poster beds and canvas tents the size of modest houses.

"I've been thinking about what we saw in West Orange." Firestone said.

"Yes," Ford chimed in. "So sorry about your house and grounds. Seeing that enemy agent dissolve into smoke was quite unnerving."

"The house and grounds can be rebuilt. The personnel cannot," Edison replied.

"Tragic. Simply tragic. How many were lost? Including the men on the train?"

"None, actually Mr. Ford." All eyes turned in surprise at the voice of Security Chief Joe

Frankel. "Four men wounded and lots of bruises but we didn't lose a single operative."

The three men had jumped to their feet and were slapping Frankels on the back, shaking his hand and staring in disbelief.

Firestone was the first to regain his voice.

"How is this possible? We went to the funerals. You, and young Fogarty, too."

"Have a seat, gentlemen, I will explain everything."

❦

February 1928

Aboard the night train

It was damnably risky to be sure but Felix got his feet pointed down and his arms crossed on his chest just as he plunged into the frigid waters of the river. He very nearly inhaled a lung full of water as the icy grip shocked his system but he managed to pull the inflator on his hidden air bladder and it worked as advertised, floating him to the surface. Three boats with shuttered searchlights scanning the surface raced toward him the moment he was spotted. When he had been plucked from the water he shrugged off his coat and the newly-developed bullet-proof vest and wrapped himself in the proffered blankets. With his teeth chattering he stuttered out a question.

"How'd it go?"

"Fine here, sir. Let's get you to shore, you can ask Ed yourself about the rest."

"Never mind, head for the debarkation point. This operation can still be blown up."

"Yes sir." The man at the helm signaled to the other boats and each one headed in a different direction as planned.

On board the train Ed and the other AEGIS bodyguards waited until the porter passed among them and gave them the all clear. Regaining their feet, they dusted themselves off and left the train when it stopped at a freight siding a few miles beyond the bridge. They scattered as planned.

CR

West Orange, New Jersey

When the last of the Silver Star agents had retreated from the scene Joe tentatively lifted his head. Without arising he softly whistled.

"It's all over, Boss." Someone shouted. "They're gone. But the West Orange Fire Brigade is on the way. I can hear the bells."

"Okay fellas, let's go." Frankels was on his feet now and yelling out instructions. "We have a lot to do, and not much time to do it."

◌◌

April 1928

Adirondack campsite

"You're telling us this was some elaborate charade?" Edison was slack-jawed at what he was hearing.

"More than that, sir, it was a complete re-ordering of our security system. Dr. Starr, myself and Eula began the initial planning when Felix was still recovering from his gunshot wound in Shanghai. Given the scope and complexity of the project Crowley was financing, we knew it would only be a matter of time before he made an effort to restart the project. Since he didn't have much left, and he wouldn't want to start over, the logical conclusion was he would mount an armed effort to steal back the technology."

"I still don't understand." Firestone scratched head. "Edison's workshop was destroyed and all the important work taken. Glenmont Manor was half destroyed by fire. Nothing has happened since then. We're only just beginning to clean up and rebuild."

"Yes, the near loss of Mr. Edison's home was unfortunate, but everything else went exactly as we hoped. Nothing taken from the workshop had any practical value, it was just an elaborate Tinker Toy setup designed to look like important work was being done. Mr. Ford, you accidentally sending our worker skyward was a theatrical bonus that helped close the deal. We suspected the janitor and when he managed to electrocute himself it had us worried. We thought we had lost our ability to feed misleading information. Then we got an intelligence report from our contact inside their operation that Major Song Li was in charge of Silver Star efforts. From there we let her anger at Fogarty blind her."

"What about the blueprints. Felix spent weeks working on those, even after he returned from China."

"The plans are fake. And by that I mean he spent a lot of effort creating plans that will require lots of time and resources to put together. And when they are done it will make lots of important sounding noises without doing anything useful at all. Felix was quite proud of himself on that score. He said everything in the diagram is critical to making everything busy. His complications all feed a circular loop that randomly selects a circuit to burn out. At their core the diagrams are for a perpetual minor failure machine."

"You mean my team has been doing useless busywork for more than a year?" Edison looked to be working himself into a full lather. "More than a year wasted when valuable research could have been underway? Why wasn't I kept informed of this?"

"Yes, and no," Frankels responded. "Yes, it was busywork in West Orange, but no, it doesn't mean no research was done. Your employees come and go, so we took advantage of that. Your best technicians drifted off and we secretly transferred them to another facility. And as far as not telling you, we didn't tell anyone who wasn't directly involved, and only when it was absolutely necessary. None of you are trained operatives and one slip of the tongue could have ruined our entire effort."

"I see it now," Harvey Firestone mused. "The dog and pony show for us was a cover story to hide that our money was actually going to this new facility somewhere. And I presume the meeting Wonder Boy was coming to in Akron was a ruse as well."

"Yes it was. In fact the entire train was an AEGIS operation. No civilians were aboard at all, no baggage or mail; only a select group of men and women in place to execute the plan."

"So where is this other secret facility?" Edison demanded.

"That's a good question. I think I'll let our expert answer that one." Frankels pointed to an object in the sky with a dozen tiny dots trailing it. Soon every eyeball in the camp was fixed on the collection in the sky.

"It's an airship!" Firestone exclaimed. "Are those fighter planes?"

The viewer's expectation of a massive airship with trailing fighters had skewed their sense of size. As it drew nearer it became clear this was a vessel a third shorter than the current *Daedalus* Class. But the astonishing element was that there was no envelope containing a lighter than air mix to hold it aloft. The objects behind were equally surprising to behold. They were best described as flying motorcycles, but without wheels, each piloted by one person wearing standard issue goggles and helmets.

Whisper quiet, the ship and air squadron deployed landing struts and settled to the ground in the meadow at the edge of the campsite. Air bike pilots stood at parade rest next to their machines and a gantry was deployed from the larger ship.

Into the springtime sun stepped Felix Fogarty and Eula Esterhaus. The two walked over to the members of the Vagabonds.

"Gentlemen," Felix began, "may I present to you the first Commander of the newly formed AEGIS special forces group *Defensores Lucem.*"

"The Defenders of the Light. I like it," Joe interjected. "Nice to see you again, Eula." She nodded an acknowledgment.

"Thank you." she responded. "And may I propose to the founders of AEGIS a new award for conspicuous gallantry in the face of the forces of evil, the Order of the Paladin and cite Felix Fogarty and Joe Frankels to become the first recipients."

"You may, Eula." Edison said. "We will take your recommendations under advisement." Turning to Fogarty he enthused, "My God, young man, it is good to see you alive and well! What is this you have brought us?"

"This is the prototype *Aeroship Athena*. I took Jeffrey Briggs original design and ran with it. No gas envelope, turbofans only for propulsion, fully self-sustaining. It can remain aloft until food and water run out for the crew using the only known operating system utilizing miniature circuitry and Lenzium repulsor technology. Each of the air riders is powered the same way."

"Fantastic! Tell us all about it. May we take a look?" The captains of industry were like kids with new toys.

"Certainly," said Felix. "Let me tell you how I met Bill Boeing and what I was doing in Seattle."

Lili LaRue and the Twisted Tracks

by Brina Williamson

Though her name was rather diminutive, Lili LaRue was anything but. At six-foot-two, she towered over most of the drivers on the racecourse, aided even more by her confident posture and patent leather pumps.

Striding forward to join the others on the starting line, her blue coveralls hugged her widest curves, as she neatly tucked her glossy, red finger waves beneath her motoring helmet.

Slipping on her gloves, Lili spotted an old friend. Two cars down, the trademark fire engine red of Clyde Bernett's Mercedes-Benz was unmistakable even before its driver approached in matching red coveralls and motoring helmet, his large goggles masking what his excessively bushy mustache didn't.

Lili chuckled. "Darling Clyde, always did like showing off."

It was Clyde who had pulled Lili into the racing circuit years ago, and the sight of his car at the starting line always assured her she was in for a healthy competition. Catching his eye with a wave, Lili saluted her old friend with a wink, to say, "may the best woman win," but instead of returning her salute in his usual, sportsmanlike way, his gaze flicked past without acknowledgment.

The announcer's voice sounded over the loudspeaker, calling for the competitors to make ready, and each driver lined up in front of their vehicle, poised and ready to run. Lili slipped on her goggles, glancing repeatedly toward Clyde, still puzzled by his behavior. The starting flag dropped and all raced for their cars.

Vaulting into her silver Bugatti type 35C Grand Prix racer, its engine roaring to life at the turn of a switch, Lili set her motor into gear. In a thunder of revving engines, the cars took off, a cloud of black fumes in their wake.

Gripping the wheel, Lili narrowed her sights down the track as several small speedsters shot out in front, but Lili paid them no mind. With 128 horsepower and superior maneuverability, she'd overtake them in no time.

Soon a speedster veered off the track, its overtaxed engine smoking as it slammed into a ditch and rolled out of sight. The racers sped past the wreck, unfazed by the all-too-common sight.

Dirt kicked up off the tracks, spraying across Lili's face and shoulders as she raced along, a smile crossing her red lips. It was a sensation only experienced on the racing circuit, and Lili lived for it.

Red flashed by on Lili's right as Clyde sped out ahead. Lili smiled, watching him move into position to slip past two competitors with one of his daring maneuvers. But, once again, Clyde was not himself, as the opening remained unseized by the normally daring driver. Drifting back, Clyde practically allowed Lili and the others to pass him.

Has something gone wrong with his car? thought Lili, before a deafening screech sounded behind her, punctuated by the roar of an explosion.

Gasps echoed among the observers, but Lili remained on course, incapable of looking back without risking her own life. The cars raced on, rounding the wide track only to spot the cleanup crew fighting the flames of the accident. Who had crashed? Lili searched the cars around her for Clyde's red Mercedes but could find no reassurance it wasn't him.

Round and round they went, forced by their sponsors to shred across the road until the final car crossed the finish line. Lili ended the race in third place, but all her thoughts remained on the flaming wreck, and her old friend's welfare.

Lili ran toward the remains of the once-flaming car, and though she hoped against it, the bright red wreckage confirmed her fears. It had been Clyde in the crash, and the small snippets of conversation among the onlookers only left a pit in Lili's stomach.

"They couldn't get him out in time."

"Burnt to a crisp, the poor sap."

CR

Lili looked over the scorched Mercedes, made partly of magnesium alloy, which had further facilitated the blaze.

"Thank you for taking a second look at her, Bill," said Lili.

"No trouble, Lili. Clyde was my friend too."

"So, did you find anything?"

Bill sighed. "It's hard to say...I found possible signs of filing on the steering column that could've caused it to snap."

"Filing?"

"Possibly. But it might also be wear and tear, exacerbated by the crash. And that's not all I found either..."

Lili struggled to hold back her impatience. "Just tell me, from everything you found, is sabotage a possibility?"

Bill hesitated. "It's a possibility, yes."

"Then why didn't you tell the police as much?"

"Because none of it's remotely conclusive. I didn't want to cast needless suspicion on the other drivers, you included."

"Me? Clyde was my friend, why in the world should the police suspect me?"

"The police always look at anyone with a connection to the victim. You would be their primary suspect, Lili."

"Well, we can't just leave it alone! Clyde wasn't himself all through the race and was far too skilled a driver to lose control of a car he was that familiar with. No, someone killed my friend, and if we can't trust the police to investigate this without bias, then I will."

"If you find anything that's more concrete, or points to who might have had a motive, we can take our findings to the police then."

Lili shook the mechanic firmly by the hand for his assistance. With Clyde's dazzling reputation in the circuit, he may have been sabotaged to give another driver an edge, but if this were the case, surely more than one car would have been tampered with. Was Clyde singled out, or had any other cars gotten the same treatment?

Before setting off, Lili requested Bill try to get access to the other cars and search for signs of sabotage while she investigated the other drivers. With the crash already labeled a tragic accident, they would need to gather as much evidence of who had a motive, if they hoped to pique the police's interest in reopening the investigation.

CR

The most likely to benefit from dispatching Clyde were the first- and second-place winners, but with only a cursory glance into their backgrounds, Lili found both men to have clear records of being well-established in the circuit as excellent competitors and would hardly risk sabotaging another man's car for a win they could easily snatch up on their own merit. Neither man had any sign of gambling addictions or outstanding debts; indeed, they both seemed to be infuriatingly upstanding fellows.

Even more infuriating was the news from Bill that he could find no evidence of sabotage on any of the cars he'd been allowed access to. Which meant it might have been Clyde himself, and not the race, which was the target, and the race had only been an easy means of killing him without raising suspicion.

With little to go on, Lili found herself rolling up to Clyde's house in search of answers. If anyone had a motive to kill him, perhaps some trace could be found in his things. Though, clearly marked letters containing explicit death threats seemed too much to hope for.

Being a woman of unladylike repute, Lili LaRue had fortunately picked up some unladylike skills, automotive expertise being at the top, but also, in this situation specifically, lock picking. With little effort, the back door creaked open, and Lili shook her head at Clyde's slack security measures. Stepping inside, it felt as though the cluttered rooms were taunting her with the hopelessness of her impending search, and Lili grumbled at Clyde's sprawling home, wishing he'd embraced even a little minimalism in his life.

Her clicking heels sounded through the lifeless house as she moved from room to room, hardly knowing what she was searching for. A journal, a threatening note, or perhaps a riddle? Around and around she went, peeking behind pillows and shaking out books as she grew increasingly exasperated with the sheer impossibility of her task.

"They make sleuthing look so easy in novels...as though clues just fall from the sky when convenient."

Stepping into the living room, Lili spotted a stack of letters laying half-covered beneath a mountain of clutter on a corner table. Pushing aside the mess, Lili slipped the envelopes out and began flipping past bills and other mundane correspondence until one marked *Neil Bernett, New York* caught her attention. It had not been the name, nor the address which had caught Lili's eye, but rather the handwriting itself, for it strongly resembled the illegible scrawl of someone she had once known well. Someone she had loved.

His name was Daniel Hashimoto, introduced to her through their mutual friend, Clyde Bernett, and from there the romance had blossomed almost instantly...at least, it had after Lili grew impatient waiting for the timid scientist to find the courage to ask her out, and had boldly invited him for a long drive along the Italian coast in her new car.

But about four years ago, in May of 1924, Daniel had vanished without a word, leaving Lili to fear all manner of ghastly possibilities, but never find satisfaction with a single answer. Now she stood, reading a seemingly innocuous letter in his hand, addressed under another name, to her dear friend Clyde, who in all these years hadn't bothered to mention he'd been in contact with her lost love.

"Oh, Clyde, I could kill you! If you weren't already dead," Lili fumed. "Why would you keep this from me? What secret were you two hiding? And is it connected to how you died?"

These questions swirled in her head, and Lili determined to root out the answers. Even if she turned out to be wrong, and the writer wasn't even Daniel, she had to follow it up and find out for sure. After all, she had an address to go on now. Pocketing the letter, Lili took a final look around the house before exiting out the back door.

Heading for her car, Lili spotted a man crossing the street toward her, and remembered him loitering there before, when she'd pulled up. As he neared, his very appearance gave Lili hesitation. A ragged scar ran down his cheek, and several silver teeth glinted in his growing smile.

"Good evening, Miss," the stranger said in a thick Boston accent, touching the brim of his black homburg.

"Evening," Lili said curtly, quickening her pace to pass him as swiftly as possible.

But the stranger stepped abruptly in her path and took hold of her arm. "Where are you going in such a hurry?"

Lili froze. As an independent woman, she had been stopped by such men more than once in her past and had learned the benefits of a solid right hook. Batting her lashes and biting her lip in feigned timidity, Lili clenched her free fist and, without a solitary word, sent the stranger's head reeling back with an abrupt uppercut to the chin.

His eyes crossed as he fell backward in a dazed stupor and, with this small window of escape, Lili bolted for her car faster than she ever had for any race. Leaping inside, her engine roared to life, and she sped down the road, a cloud of fumes in her wake.

Lying unconscious on the sidewalk, Lili's would-be attacker's skin began to sizzle, this vital clue and inexplicable event going unseen by the world around, until his body had fully disintegrated.

⊙♥

With an overnight bag packed and stowed in the boot of her Mercedes Torpedo Roadster, Lili headed to New York in search of answers. Wind whipped across her face, her cloche hat shielding her perfect finger waves from becoming a tousled mess, not that she would've cared in the slightest if they had been. She was enjoying the hours on the road; it was where she was most at home.

The sun flashed and flickered through the trees alongside her, and Lili drank in the atmosphere, but her enjoyment ceased when a distinct black car began drifting into her rear view mirror. More than once, a vehicle crept into view behind her, only to vanish out of sight for a time before returning to follow at a distance for another lengthy stretch of road.

To anyone else, it might have seemed like any old black car, but Lili recognized the make as a Chrysler Imperial, and knew it was the same car each time it reappeared. Someone was tailing her. The road stretched out ahead with no visible turns to utilize, but Lili was patient, keeping close track of the car behind her as she bided her time, cautious not to let on that she'd spotted them.

At last, the moment came to make her move when a clear side road breaking off into a distant town came into view ahead. Slowing near the turn, Lili pulled off to the side of the road, and took a map from her glove box, sticking her nose behind it and giving her pursuers no option but to pass by, or risk showing their hand.

Awaiting the roll of their passing wheels, Lili peeked in her rear view mirror to find that they too had pulled to the side of the road some yards behind her. Gritting her teeth, Lili refolded her map and clutched the wheel of her car. If there was one thing Lili knew how to do well, it was to drive fast, with expert control, and if ever there was a time to utilize her skills, it was now.

With a roll of her shoulders, she shifted into gear and shot from the curb, the idling tail falling swiftly behind as they struggled to catch up. With a tight turn, Lili bolted down the side road as the Chrysler raced to close the rapidly growing distance between them.

Veering down another side street, Lili shifted gears, picking up speed as her tail struggled to round the sharp corner in pursuit.

Faster and faster she sped, rounding turn after turn to build the growing gap.

Breaking out onto a two-lane road, an opportunity presented itself to lose her tail completely. Lili waited until the last moment, a skip between two heartbeats, before launching her car into a hard spin across both lanes to tear down a side road going in the opposite direction. With little time to turn, and another car fast approaching, the Chrysler veered off the road in its attempt to follow, plowing into a ditch.

Lili laughed a little as they struggled to recover, tempted to toy with them before losing them completely, but reason won out, and she pushed her car to its limits, turning down every side street she could utilize until her tail was completely out of view. Slipping down another side street, Lili breathed a deep, satisfied sigh. She'd lost them.

જ

Lili checked and rechecked the address on the envelope, unsure if she had the right place. But it was no mistake, this crumbling brick building was it. This was where she would find answers. She hoped so, at least.

Hesitating to approach the front door, Lili thought it best to first look around and perhaps peer inside a window or two, just to be thorough. But the windows presented little peering opportunity, as they were all long overdue for a ruthless cleaning.

Rounding the back, she spied a small patch of window, which offered a mostly clear view inside, and bent close. Lili cupped her hands around her eyes to block out the light. Inside, tables and chairs sat neatly arranged in the center of the room, while several shelves filled with books, binders, bottles, and other assorted devices, were lined up along most available wall space. Yet with how well-maintained the interior looked in contrast to the exterior, there still seemed no sign of life stirring within. Grabbing a rag off a nearby junk pile, Lili wiped the window as clean as she could, for a better look inside, but as she bent closer to peer in once more, a face stared back at her, eyes wide in stunned surprise.

"Daniel!" Lili cried.

On the other side of the glass were her long-lost love's unmistakable features: his full lips, deep brown eyes, glossy black hair, and olive skin. He was just as handsome as Lili remembered, if not more so.

Untold moments passed in silent shock, before at last Daniel stepped forward and opened the window. "Lili? What... how?" Daniel's voice cracked. "How on earth are you here?"

"I...I found your letter..." Lili said, all usual confidence completely absent from her voice.

"My letter?"

"Yes. The one you sent to Clyde under another name. I recognized your handwriting."

"What were you doing going through Clyde's mail?"

"I was looking for...hold on a minute," Lili planted her fists decisively on her hips. "You disappeared! I thought you were dead! After all these years of silence, where do you get the gall to question me?"

"I'm sorry, I wanted to explain before I left, but I thought it might put you in danger. You must believe that I only did it to keep you safe."

"Danger? Daniel, what is going on? Why are you writing to Clyde under another name, why are you hiding in this crumbling wreck of a building, and why haven't you invited me in yet?"

"Well, it's all rather complicated—" Daniel cut himself off, finally registering Lili's last question. "Oh, yes, of course, come in."

Pushing the window fully open, he stepped politely back to give her room.

"What is the matter with you? I'm not climbing through there."

Daniel hesitated, flustered by the increasingly awkward situation. "Well, where would you...should I help you through?"

"No, Daniel, where's the back door?"

"Oh, right!" he stammered, stepping out of sight without any indication of which way she should go to be let in.

"Oh, this is intolerable," Lili muttered, vaulting up onto the windowsill to climb unceremoniously inside.

Returning, Daniel apologized repeatedly for the awkward reintroduction.

"This is truly not how I envisioned us meeting again," Daniel said, taking Lili's hand to help her into the building.

"So, you thought about that, did you?"

"Every day."

Lili flushed at his words. "Then you did plan to...return?"

"I hoped to."

Lili looked into his eyes, feeling her resolve to be angry with him beginning to weaken.

"No," she spat, pulling away. "I'm not forgiving you that easily. You abandoned me without a word for four years, got Clyde mixed up in whatever all this danger is, and now he's dead, likely because of you!"

"Clyde...dead? But how?"

"Someone tampered with his car before our race, and he lost control."

"And you think it's connected to me?"

"I don't know for sure. But none of the other drivers had a real motive, and now you're telling me you're mixed up in something dangerous... it's not exactly a tremendous leap. Just what have you both gotten involved in?"

Daniel shook his head, slumping into a nearby chair. "I genuinely don't know. Four years ago, my mind was on only two things... my research, and you. The more I knew you, the more innovations I seemed to make," Daniel reminisced. "You were like the muse to my experiments."

Lili blushed once more at the memories.

"But in my excitement, I made the mistake of telling one too many people of the breakthroughs in my research and, more importantly, the militaristic potential of my work. Within weeks, I had three separate men come knock-ing on my door: one claimed to be from an agency called AEGIS, while the others were with independent investors, all of which were interested in funding my research in exchange for exclusive rights. At first, I thought my ship had come in, men were competing to fund my work. But when my apartment was ransacked, and my research papers rifled, I knew one of them must be behind it. Something about the first man set me on edge from the start... he smiled too much and looked nothing like a man of science should... more like a gangster's goon with his scar and silver teeth."

Lili perked up. "Silver teeth?"

"Yes, several of them."

"Did he have a Boston accent?"

"Yes...how did you know that?"

"Because I think I socked your goon on the chin, just outside Clyde's home!"

Daniel shot from his seat, grabbing Lili by the shoulders. "Lili, are you sure?"

"I'm positive."

"Did he follow you?"

"He didn't, but someone was tailing me on my way here, to find you."

"What?"

"It's all right, don't worry, I lost them."

As if on cue, the windows burst in from all sides, as three men in long, black overcoats came crashing inside.

Lili blinked in astonishment. "At least...I thought I lost them."

A length of rope was stretched taught between one man's hands, while another pulled a bottle and rag from his pockets.

The third man leveled a pistol toward them. "Don't move!"

Daniel raised his hands. "Don't shoot, I'll come willingly. There's no need for anyone to get hurt."

Lili gripped Daniel's arm. "Daniel, what are you doing?" she whispered.

"Trying to save our necks."

Pulling free of her grasp, Daniel stepped slowly forward in surrender. The man with the rope stepped up to restrain him, but Daniel leaped to the side, grabbing a bottle off a shelf and shattering it on the floor. The contents burst into colorful smoke, filling the room in moments, and all occupants' eyes with tears.

Bullets whizzed through the air, before a voice shouted, "Stop! Ziegler said to take him alive!"

Lili ducked, coughing, and shielding her face in her sleeve to little effect. A hand grabbed hold of Lili's arm and, without thinking, she threw a right hook toward her assailant.

He grunted in pain, before hissing, "Stop! It's me, Daniel! This way."

Crouching behind the furniture, Lili held tight to Daniel's jacket as he led her on. The three invaders shouted behind the fog, their shadows moving through the haze to uncover their targets.

All at once, hands grabbed hold of Lili from behind, and she cried out as they wrenched her away from Daniel. Spinning around, she landed a devastating blow to her attacker's chin, sending him reeling backward to the floor.

Turning, Lili spotted Daniel in the fog calling out to her, "Lili, this way!"

But before she could reach him, a pair of hands grappled Daniel from behind, covering his mouth with a damp rag and pulling him into the haze.

"Daniel!" Lili cried, racing after him.

The shadows of the two figures wavered in and out of sight as Lili squinted to see them in the stinging fog, their shapes quickly vanishing through a glowing void ahead. Following, she found the broken window they had escaped by and clambered out into the open.

Not taking even a moment to breathe the fresh air, Lili spotted Daniel's abductors dragging his limp body out of sight around the building and raced after them. As Lili reached the corner, three shots cracked against the brick wall and forced her back, behind cover.

Knowing she had no way of overwhelming two armed men by herself, Lili waited behind the wall for the conflict to move to her playground: the road. The men scrambled into their car, shoving Daniel inside before peeling away from the curb with uncontrolled recklessness.

"Amateurs," Lili muttered, bolting for her car the moment they had sped off.

Leaping into the driver's seat, Lili shot from the curb with record speed. She felt a rush of energy identical to starting a race, but her desire to win was for neither thrill nor money; she was racing to save a life, the life of a man, she hated to admit, she still loved.

☙

Lili held back, just out of sight, as she tailed the Chrysler Imperial which Daniel was now trapped inside. She couldn't risk being seen for even a second; these men had tailed her here and would instantly recognize her distinctive car. With no means of saving Daniel while he was in the hands of two hefty goons, she hoped whoever held him might let their guard down, even just a little, once they reached their destination, and leave Daniel on his own, giving her a chance to slip in and extricate him.

Lili maintained her speed, out of sight behind any car that offered her cover, but as the streets grew isolated and empty, Lili was forced to fall back even further. It felt as though they'd driven for miles before Lili spotted a distant mansion, silhouetted against the setting sun. The road which curved through the hills seemed to be leading straight toward it, and Lili knew it was their intended destination.

Slowing, Lili pulled off to the side of the road as the Chrysler Imperial turned up ahead into the long drive toward the mansion. Alighting from her car, Lili crept through the mansion grounds, climbing over a low fence and ducking behind a tree as she inched ever closer to the structure. The Chrysler pulled up into the circular drive out front and the two hefty thugs emerged, pulling a half-conscious

Daniel out of the car, and escorting him inside, his limp feet dragging in the gravel.

Lili held back, watching, and biding her time as lights flicked on and off within the mansion. Finally, a light switched on in a main floor room, and foggy shadows of three figures moved beyond the curtain within. One man coldly struck a backhanded blow across another's face and the shadows lingered for a moment longer, until the light was switched off, and all was plunged into darkness.

Lili felt sure the man who'd been struck was Daniel, and crept toward the solitary window. A sudden crunch of dry leaves and murmur of voices sent her ducking behind a tree as two armed men tramped by, most likely on a patrol of the grounds for intruders like herself.

With the danger passed, Lili crept closer, slipping unnoticed up to the room where Daniel was being held. Peering inside through the crack in the curtain, Lili could just make out the room from the sliver of light which radiated beneath the door, and Daniel's unconscious form lying on a bed, his hands and feet tied securely to the bedposts.

Eager to free him from his restraints, Lili pushed against the window but, as she should have predicted, it was locked tight. Muttering at yet another obstacle barring her path, Lili spotted an abandoned trowel in a nearby garden and snatched it up, soon prying the window open with a little muscle and ingenuity.

There he lay, motionless, and bound on the bed as Lili tiptoed toward him, whispering his name as she neared. "Daniel? Daniel, are you awake? I've come to get you out of here."

He shifted, groaning faintly as Lili went to work untying his hands, but as he turned to look at her, she gasped at the sight of his face.

"It can't be...Clyde?"

"Lili?" Clyde muttered through a split lip. One eye was half swollen shut but, sure enough, it was Clyde, alive and most definitely not burnt to a crisp.

"Clyde, you're alive?!"

"Shush! They'll hear you," Clyde whispered.

"But, I saw you crash," Lili said, still in disbelief. "How did you get out alive?"

"Crash? What crash?"

"In the race, six days ago."

"I never made it to any race. I've been here for the last two weeks."

"Then who was the man driving your car?"

"How should I know?"

Lili's eyes went wide as the puzzle pieces finally fell into place. "A double. They sent a double and rigged it so he'd be killed as you, and no one would ever come looking for you!"

"Will you please lower your voice," Clyde hissed, "and untie me already?"

Lili bit her lip, apologizing repeatedly as she loosened his restraints until at last he was free and on his feet.

"So, what's the escape plan?" Clyde asked, rubbing his wrists.

"We can't. Not yet."

"Why not?"

"They still have Daniel."

"What? How? When? I didn't tell them anything. How could they possibly...?"

Lili bit her lip again. "I might have led them to him."

Clyde fumed. "You? How did you even find him? Oh, never mind. We've got to get him away from them."

"But how? We don't even know where they're keeping him."

Clyde sat on the bed, stroking his mustache in thought but, just then, footsteps sounded outside.

"Quick," Clyde whispered, "Under the bed, someone's coming."

Scrambling beneath the cramped bed, Lili struggled to keep her long legs tucked out of sight, as Clyde lay back on the mattress above, wrapping the ropes loosely around his feet and wrists before a key turned in the lock of the door.

A tall man stepped inside, light from the hall outside silhouetted his lanky figure, illuminating fiery red hair beneath his low hat.

"All right, Bernett," said the thug in a sharp, creaking voice, "time to make yourself useful. We've got a friend who's come to visit you."

Lili watched as the man's large feet approached, leaning in to extract Clyde from his bonds. There'd been no time before for the exchange of plans, so Lili could only hope her next action was the right one.

Launching her long leg out from beneath the bed, Lili swept across the man's ankles, knocking him off his feet with a single kick. The thug came thudding to the ground and Clyde leapt from the bed, grabbing hold of his arms as he struggled to resist.

"Grab his gun!" Clyde spat.

Lili scrambled out and tugged the pistol from the holster at the thug's hip. She leveled the gun at the goon, hissing for him to put his hands up.

"Do it, or I'll shoot!"

Not a moment's notice was given to her, as the two men continued to grapple on the floor. Lili *harumphed*, turning the gun in her grip, and thwacking the thug across the temple with the butt as his head came in reach. He slumped unconscious to the floor, and Clyde sat back, catching his breath for a moment, and nodding in gratitude toward Lili.

"Now what?" Lili asked. "How do we find Daniel?"

"Let me catch my breath for a moment, woman."

"But they could be torturing him."

"No, I don't think so. This fellow said something as he walked in...something about making myself useful, and a visitor. I think they were going to take me to Dan and use me to make him...more cooperative."

"Well, it's too bad we just knocked out your escort. They would've taken us right to him!"

Clyde looked down at the body, starting to formulate something. "We might be able to salvage it. How tall are you?"

Lili raised an eyebrow, as if her towering height wasn't common knowledge to all who knew her.

"Just help me get this guy out of his clothes, will you?" said Clyde.

"I beg your pardon?"

Clyde reached for the limp body's jacket when a sudden sizzling sent him reeling back. The body had begun to dissolve before their very eyes!

"What in Heaven's name? Who are these people?" said Lili.

"I'm not sure... but I remember overhearing mentions of occult powers, and an agency called Silver Star, when they thought I wasn't listening."

"Occult powers?"

The two watched, mouths agape, as the man's flesh bubbled and burnt away into nothing but bones, which shortly followed, crumbling into dust and leaving behind nothing save an empty suit.

"Well..." Lili said, still blinking in disbelief. "You wanted to get his suit off."

CR

The tall, fiery-haired thug held Clyde tightly by the arm, pushing him from the room, pistol drawn.

"Ow," Clyde muttered. "You don't have to twist my arm like that."

"Sorry," Lili whispered, pulling down her cap and tugging up the collar of her newly-donned jacket to conceal her face.

Clyde glanced back at her and grimaced. "Wipe off that lipstick, will you?"

Lili pulled the handkerchief from her pocket and dabbed her red lips with haste.

"Better?" she asked.

Clyde crinkled his nose at the pink stain now lining her lips. "Marginally."

Continuing down the hall, Clyde directed Lili toward the room he'd last been questioned in but, as they approached, a gruff voice called out from upstairs.

"Where do you think you're taking him?"

Lili glanced up before swiftly concealing her face beneath her hat brim. "To the... umm..."

"Library," Clyde whispered.

"To the library," Lili called back, struggling to mimic the creaky voice that had belonged to the suit's previous owner.

"What you taking him there for? Boss wants him up in the blue room, with that Hashimo fellow."

"Right," Lili said, nodding behind her hat brim. "Where's the blue room?" she whispered to Clyde.

"Search me."

"Oh, a great help you are."

Jabbing the pistol dramatically in his ribs, Lili pushed Clyde up the long curving staircase, reaching the landing and turning right, her fingers securely crossed.

"Left, you idiot!" spat the thug on the balcony across from them. "Four doors down."

"Right," Lili muttered. "Forgot."

Turning left, Lili spotted light trailing out across the carpet from a door slightly ajar, exactly four rooms down. Taking in a deep, anxious breath as she approached, Lili kicked open the door to find a grim scene.

A single lamp illuminated the center of the room where Daniel sat, tied to a chair, flanked by two men, whose suits seemed ill-equipped to contain their bulging muscles. To the left, mixing a drink at a small table, was a lean, bespectacled man, who glanced vaguely toward them as they entered.

"Take a seat, Mr. Bernett," he said, nodding at an empty chair opposite Daniel.

Lili hesitated only a moment before shoving Clyde roughly into the chair. Picking up a length of cord which lay on the ground, she contrived restraining Clyde's hands behind his back in such a way that the knots would give when the time was right.

"Daniel," Clyde whispered. "Are you all right?"

Daniel looked up, still obviously groggy from whatever had been used to knock him out, but his eyes shot open at the sight of Clyde, who he'd believed to be dead.

"Clyde? You're...you're alive?" Daniel gasped.

"Sure, I am, buddy. You can't be rid of me that easy."

"I hate to interrupt," the bespectacled man said in a thick German accent. "But we have business to discuss."

"We aren't saying a word to you, Ziegler!" Clyde spat.

"Hmmm... yes, well, fortunately, your stubbornness won't be a thorn in my side any longer, since my men found your friend without your help, anyway. No, you, Mr. Bernett, will have a new role of motivator for your friend to be... cooperative."

Daniel swallowed nervously, as Ziegler leaned toward him with his last words. Straightening up to adjust his spectacles, Ziegler casually sipped his drink, turning back to the table which Lili now noticed held a neat row of sharp implements.

Lili stood up next to Clyde, her head bowed behind her cap brim as she shifted out of the light's reach, pistol drawn and waiting to make her move.

"What shall we start with...?" Ziegler said in a singsong voice, running his fingers across the implements of torture.

Clyde looked reassuringly at Daniel, his eyes glancing repeatedly toward Lili the moment their captors weren't looking. At first Daniel only raised an eyebrow at him, until the hand of Clyde's guard caught his attention; specifically, her long red nails. His eyes trailed up to the towering thug's soft face, and Lili gave him a sly wink, mouthing the words, "get ready."

In the next moment, Clyde charged, tossing aside his loose ropes and tackling the thug at Daniel's right. The second goon reached for his weapon, but Lili stepped in, clonking him over the head with the butt of her pistol and sending him crashing to the ground. With a little assistance from the threat of Lili's pistol, Clyde soon confiscated the other thug's gun, and both leveled their firearms at Ziegler and his goon.

"Go on," Clyde hissed, shooing them toward the back of the room as Lili loosened Daniel's bonds. "Hands up and face down on the ground. And don't even think about calling for help."

"You're not going to get away," said Ziegler. "You shoot that gun, and all my men will be down on you in seconds."

"And if I don't, you'll send them after us the second there's no gun to your head."

Ziegler smiled up from the ground. "Like I said...you're trapped."

"Guess I'll have to find a third option."

With that, Clyde cracked his gun across the two men's temples, sending them slumping limply to the floor. Helping Daniel out of his restraints, they raced to the door. Peering carefully out, Lili saw no one within view, but could make out voices in the entry hall below.

"Sounds like they're really giving those guys a beating upstairs," said one voice.

"I'll say. I think a chair got knocked over," said another

"Hall is all clear," Lili whispered. "But there are at least two men downstairs."

"There's a back staircase," said Clyde. "They made me use it once, when some salesman came to the door."

Daniel and Lili nodded.

"Lead the way."

Slipping silently out into the hall, they crept behind Clyde toward the back spiral staircase but, as they neared, a looming shadow began ascending the stairs. Pulling back, they ducked inside an unoccupied room, hearts pounding as the man reached the top.

Through the tiny crack in the door, Lili waited as the man proceeded down the hall, mercifully oblivious to their presence as he turned a corner out of view, and they could at last slip unnoticed down the stairs.

Reaching the bottom, a sound of alarm exploded behind them. "They've escaped!" A booming voice echoed through the house. "They took out Ziegler and escaped!"

Clyde raced for a window and threw it open, allowing the trio to scramble outside just as another distant voice echoed behind them.

"Get the dogs and search the grounds! They must be found!"

Racing across the side lawn, they hoped to cover as much ground as possible before their pursuers could mobilize, but Lili halted, spotting the car on the front driveway.

"Lili, come on!" Daniel and Clyde called to her as they reached a cluster of trees.

Steadying her pistol, Lili squeezed off two, well-placed shots, bursting two tires of the Chrysler Imperial before racing for the trees.

"Brilliant! Now they'll know exactly where we are," Clyde grumbled.

"You'll thank me later."

Rushing through the woods, shots sounded to their left, as bullets snapped amid the trees around them.

"Told you!" Clyde bellowed, ducking behind a tree to return fire on the patrolmen.

With Clyde covering their escape, Daniel and Lili sprinted toward the fence. Lili dropped behind a tree stump, cracking off several more shots toward the thugs to provide cover for Clyde's escape, and Daniel as he vaulted over the fence.

"Clyde, hurry!" Lili cried, shooting off her last rounds as he reached her.

Bullets shattered near them as they clambered over the fence and spotted Lili's Torpedo Roadster only a short way off. Sprinting for the vehicle, Lili's long legs took her a stride or two ahead of Clyde and Daniel, and she leaped into the driver's seat, revving the engine to life before they crowded into the seat beside her.

Peeling out down the road, Lili smiled, not only enjoying the speed but the knowledge that their pursuers would have rather a difficult time tailing them, with two flat tires. All view of the mansion and its sprawling grounds at last vanished behind them, and the three friends breathed in the air, relieved, yet still in disbelief at their lucky escape.

They weren't sure how long or how far they drove before at last coming to a stop on the side of the road to assess their next course of action. But as the two men stood by the parked car, poring over the map, Lili could hold in her years of emotions no longer. Stepping forward, she clenched her fist before stretching her fingers and landing a firm slap across both men's cheeks. Clyde and Daniel held their faces, staring at her in complete shock.

"What was that for?" the men said in unison.

"For keeping me in the dark! Next time, tell me you've got magic, dissolving fanatics after you before you go and get yourselves killed!"

Clyde and Daniel started to protest, but Lili struck them both silent as a new emotion took hold, and she grabbed Daniel by the face to plant a long-overdue kiss.

As the long-lost sweethearts embraced, Clyde rubbed his red cheek and muttered, "Oh sure, he abandoned you for *years*, while I just spent weeks being pummeled, biting my tongue to keep him alive, but he gets a kiss and I just get a slap. That's fair."

Walks with Bones

by Martin Shannon

Suzy ran a wet rag over the counter for what had to be the millionth time. Her consistent polishing had pulled out the occasional coffee stains, but it couldn't touch the anxiety. It did nothing for that feeling deep in the pit of her stomach that said if you don't make enough in tips then your grandfather doesn't get his pills.

It felt like that feeling would never go away.

Suzy shuddered to think about him with the pills, but worried even more about him without them.

Coffee dripped into a nearby pot, the tarry black liquid and pies sitting behind glass just about the only things this lousy diner was known for.

That, and being too close to the charter.

Suzy didn't talk about the charter, not because customers didn't want to, but because she wasn't keen on them picking up on her accent.

It would not do to hear the Blackfoot in her words.

She hadn't given Mr. Miller a fake name for nothing. It was hard enough to get work, but next to impossible if they thought you were a native.

"I'm telling you, they got magic out there, Suzy." That was Gerry, a trucker, one of the few long haulers that lingered here on his trips across the state. He was a frail man, his old body propped up by spit and coffee in equal measure. Long fingers clutched the sides of his mug as if the bones beneath them wanted nothing more than to drink the heady elixir.

She nodded.

It was best not to argue with the old man, not when he got going. He'd had a few run-ins with some local teens a couple years ago. They were good kids, for the most part, but they couldn't pass up the chance to give him a scare he'd never forgotten.

"I saw it, you know. I saw those coyote bones get right up and walk around."

There aren't any coyotes around here.

Suzy nodded again, gently, like those silly glass birds that pretend to drink the colored water. That's what she was, a bird that drank whatever they told her. She took down their praise and their hate in equal measure. She did all of that to keep the job.

She'd do near anything to keep the job.

Suzy tossed the rag in a bin under the counter, then turned her attention to the furthest booth. The old guy seated there was her only other customer tonight, and since she'd dropped off his coffee, he'd barely moved to touch it.

Leathery skin and long dark hair, he was old blood, one of the early ones. Decorum would have dictated more respect, but it also would have taken the young woman out of her disguise.

She wasn't speaking her native language, never around Gerry.

She left the coffee-clutching trucker to his quiet rantings and slipped out from behind the counter, those stupid heels clicking on the hard floor. Mr. Miller insisted that all the girls wear heels, along with the same polka dot aprons and pencil skirts. None of it felt remotely practical, but Suzy had the impression it wasn't so much for practicality as it was for making the patrons happy—the male patrons.

They were pretty much the only ones that made it this far down the highway after dark.

Suzy grabbed the pot as she clicked past, aiming to refill his mug before asking him for the tenth time if there was anything else he wanted.

Coffee in hand, the raven-haired waitress leaned over the table, aiming for his mug. "Can I get you anything, or just the coffee?"

Dressed in an ill-fitting suit and not much for conversation, he placed a hand over the mug before she could add to its rapidly cooling contents. "Your name."

She tapped a finger on her name tag, the same one Mr. Miller insisted they wear. "Suzy, says so right on my—"

"No. Your *real* name."

Suzy hazarded a glance at Gerry, but the long hauler was too busy telling the creamer all about his last run-in with Blackfoot teens to be paying any attention to the two of them.

"We don't talk about those things here."

"Why not?" Dark eyes like the cold coffee in his cup stared back at her.

"Because I've got a sick grandfather and need this job. This job pays money, and money means pills."

He frowned and dug into his coat pocket, turning the contents over in his fingers. "You don't need their medicine. It has no heart."

Suzy did her best to not dump the rest of the pot in the man's lap right then and there. She'd had enough of that from her grandfather, she didn't need it from yet another old man who thought he knew something.

The white man's medicine might be cold and sterile, but it worked against the white man's stupid diseases, or at least most of the time. She'd tried all the old cures. They hadn't worked. They'd only made him worse. She had no stomach for rehashing it again.

"The pills work."

Suzy was content to leave it at that, turning away coffee in hand and secretly hoping he'd see himself out.

Hot fingers on her wrist stopped all that dead in its tracks.

"You need real medicine. Not those sterile droppings from some metal machine. Your ancestors understood that. You need—"

She'd had it. She'd had all she could take from men telling her what was right and what was wrong. Suzy slammed the metal pot down and pulled her hand free. "I'll tell you what I need. I need a break. I don't need stories about my ancestors. I don't need myths about a world that looks nothing like this one. Spirits and the Camp of the Ghosts, I don't need them. You know what I do need? I do need one night where I get to sleep more than a couple of hours before I have to get him up to take his pills." She pulled on the edges of Mr. Miller's stupid apron. "I need a job that doesn't dress me up like a doll and make me parade around in clown shoes. I need a lot of things, what I *don't* need is some old man sitting in my diner dangling a bag of tobacco and turkey bones and telling me it will help my grandfather."

He opened his mouth to say something, but Suzy was on a roll, and as her late grandmother would have said, you never stop a thunderbird when she's bringing the lightning.

"Can you do that? Can you fix all those things? I don't think you can." She pointed at the small leather bag that had miraculously appeared in his fingers. "Unless that has gold nuggets in it, it's entirely and completely useless to me. Now, what can I get you?"

The last sentence came out with a practiced charm she wanted to yank back, skin, and hang on the drying line, but what was done was done and all she could do was force a pretend smile.

He said nothing.

Bright headlights flooded the diner glass as three cars rolled up out front.

We're going to need more coffee.

Again, Suzy turned back to the counter, but this time the old man pulled her back harder. She was just about ready to swing that coffee pot into his head and tell Mr. Miller he'd tried to get a hand under her skirt but didn't quite get there.

He shoved that leather bundle into her free hand, pushing her fingers closed around the soft deer skin.

"I told you. I don't want your—"

"Keep it safe and leave. Leave now."

Shapes moved outside the diner, tall shapes, men with dark suits and wide hats. She couldn't make out much more than that, but whoever these guys were, they didn't look like they were here for the coffee or the pie.

"What are you talking about?"

He slipped a second hand out, wrapping it around the metal pot's handle. "Leave the pot."

"Uh... right." Suzy backed away slowly, retreating to the safety of the counter and Gerry's mutterings.

"Just like that." The delivery driver squeezed a wadded-up napkin in his sausage fingers. "He rubbed it right up against the bones and 'boom' just like that they were up and moving around. And that's not all, Suzy, they had eyes. Bright eyes, red like furnace coals."

"That's nice, Gerry."

The door swung open and men poured in. It felt like that time Mr. Miller had accidentally cut the bottom of the coffee bean bag. That had been a mess, and Suzy had the feeling this was about to be a lot worse. Two at a time, they flooded the diner, swarming around the old man's booth, and doing nothing to hide their less-than-cordial intentions.

One of the larger ones slipped into the seat opposite the old man. "You know what we want. Give it to us, and we'll make this quick."

"Yes. Yes." He held up the pot. "You want coffee, right?"

A pistol emerged from the large man's jacket. "Don't waste my time, old man. Give it to me now, or I'll pull this trigger and use it on you."

Suzy froze, stuck behind the counter and not sure what to do.

Gerry didn't appear to suffer from such indecision. He slipped off the stool and put an arm around the closest man's shoulder. "I'm with you. These people are nothing but prob —"

Boom!

Gerry never finished his sentence, a bullet from the tall man's gun taking his life and his words in a single breath. Smoke drifted from the barrel, rolling gently over the big man's pale skin. "Give it to me now, or the girl gets the next bullet."

Suzy squeezed the medicine bag in her fingers. "I have it. I have what you want. Don't shoot him. Don't shoot me. I'll give it to you, I promise."

The tall man trained his weapon back on the old man. "See? I knew this could be easy."

Suzy held up the bag, waving it like a white flag. "It's right here."

"Excellent."

The old man gave her a look. It was the same sort of look her grandfather used each time she put the apron on and the fake name tag.

Disappointment.

It was also the last look he ever gave any-one.

Boom!

"Give it to me."

The tall man used his still-smoking pistol to coax Suzy to the table.

She'd seen her share of guns, but never like this. They say trauma changes a person, fight or flight. Suzy wanted both, and in equal measure. She wanted to punch that man in his angled jaw, and she also wanted to run for the parking lot, not stopping until her feet gave out.

Turns out her feet gave out a lot quicker than she expected.

Half-way across the floor, she slipped in the blood, coming down hard on what had been Gerry. Suzy used a hand to stop herself, but it happened to be the same one that held the bag.

Leather mixed with blood and something inside those soft folds cracked against the middle-aged man's ribs.

I'm sorry, Gerry.

Suzy was sorry for a lot of things. For not running, for ignoring the crazy man under her arm, and for having woken up this morning.

Strong hands grabbed her and dragged her off the still prone body of the former trucker.

"Bring her to me."

"Hey! Get your hands off me." Suzy tried to pull her arms free, but to no avail.

The man with the gun squinted at her name tag. "Suzy, is it? Funny. You don't look like a Suzy."

"Here!" She held a hand up, the partially crumpled bag locked in those bloody fingers. "You want the bag. Take it. Take it and get out of my diner. Get the hell out of my diner."

Something moved in the bag, like a worm on the hook twisting to avoid the fish's mouth. Whatever it was, it startled her, and she almost dropped it altogether.

"What was tha—" Those were all the words Suzy got out before the diner descended into chaos.

These sorts of things tend to happen when dead people get back up.

Gerry moved like a man possessed. His pale skin catching the overhead light and showing off that mortal wound, which no longer seemed to bother him in the slightest. A faint red glow twinkled from behind milky eyes. He might not have been super-coordinated, but he knew how to swing his arms and how to eat bullets.

Suzy hit the floor as gunshots rang out overhead. Suited men fired shot after shot, each one taking a chunk of flesh, but none of them stopping Gerry in the slightest. For a man who couldn't have been bothered to lift a finger most days, in death he was quite helpful.

The dead thing shrugged off the tearing metal, wrapping his fingers around a booth table and ripping it free. The tall man scrambled to get a few more pistol shots off before Gerry got a hold of his neck.

Slugs of metal ripped through flesh and bone, embedding themselves deep in a corpse that didn't appear to care.

Crack!

Gerry's fingers snapped his neck and tossed the rest of that jerk through the window. He landed somewhere on the sidewalk, very much dead.

Boom! Boom!

Suzy scrambled for the counter, crawling over fallen men and past still-smoking pistols, while above her Gerry did exactly what she wanted.

She wanted them out of her diner, and that's what he did. The thing that had been Gerry just kept coming, just kept breaking necks, eating bullets, and throwing men out the broken window.

It wasn't until the last of them ended up in a pile on the bloodstained sidewalk that Suzy stopped to catch her breath, and Gerry crumpled to the ground where he stood. The man collapsed like a folding chair, landing in a heap among the broken glass and ruined table.

Suzy didn't have time to process it, or to make sense of much of anything, before one of the car doors opened.

Long and elegant legs slipped out, legs encased in tight pants that put her uniform to shame. They traced their way up to a slender jacket with ample buttons that looked almost military. Suzy'd met a few of the guys when they'd come in from the base. If this was an army girl, it wasn't one of ours.

Run!

She wanted to. She wanted to kick those heels off and make a break for the back, but something about how this woman moved made Suzy think that would be a bad idea. Growing up on the reservation, she'd stepped on a hornet nest once, those bright yellow insects stung her no less than a few dozen times before she'd gotten away.

She'd ended up spending a night under the almost constant watchful eyes of her grandfather and coated in some pasty concoction he'd cooked up. That whole night had been just a non-stop fever dream of stingers and pain.

This woman moved like one of those hornets, mesmerizing and powerful, and most likely with a stinger to match.

Suzy clutched the tiny bag tight in her bloody fingers, the counter between her and the deadly woman practically floating through the front door.

Her long blond hair was done up in a tight bun, almost like the nest Suzy imagined her springing forth from. She popped a beret off her head and placed the black thing on the closest table before surveying Gerry's handiwork. "Impressive. I told him it would work."

Suzy held the bag up. "Get out of my diner!"

Unlike last time, Gerry didn't move. He didn't get up and toss that slender woman out on her backside. No. Gerry stayed very much unmoving, and by the looks of it, very much dead.

"I'm afraid it doesn't work that way—" The blond squinted at her name tag. "Suzy, is it? Yeah. It doesn't work that way at all."

"Gerry, get up! Get up and throw her out of my diner!"

The old trucker didn't budge.

The blond woman picked up her hat and tucked it under a jacket-covered arm. "I told you, Suzy. It doesn't work that way. Here's what's going to happen. I'll spell it out for you because the education system in this country is borderline deplorable. Don't worry, I'll use small and simple words. You're going to give that to me before things get worse for you, a lot worse."

Suzy pulled the bag back, clutching it to her blood-stained chest. "No."

"I figured you'd say that. Let me take a minute to explain. You see Gerry over there?" The blond tilted her head at the trucker gone undead bouncer. "That cost you a lot."

"Cost me—"

"Oh yes, very much, I'm afraid. Can you feel it yet? The squeezing in your chest. I'm told it's a little like having your hand stuck in a vise."

Suzy pressed the bag against her top, and the heart that beat like a tribal drum beneath it. "I'm fine."

"Sure you are, but the damage has been done. The longer you hold that thing, the worse it's going to get for you. Good chance you'll end up like Gerry here. Is that what you want?"

"I..."

The blond shook her head, moving like a rattler, slipping between the dead men and broken glass until she'd positioned herself over the former trucker. "Let's ask Gerry, shall we?"

She pulled him over, exposing that bloody face and dead eyes. Suzy's stomach rolled as if catching up with the grisly situation just now.

"Gerry?" The blond drew him up, placing her lips on his forehead and leaving a soft kiss on that pale skin. "Tell her, Gerry. Tell her what she has to do."

The old trucker screamed, his mouth open wide in agony. "Suzy! Suzy, it hurts! It hurts so much. Please make it stop. Please!"

"Gerry, I—"

"Please! I'm sorry. I'm sorry for everything. I'm sorry for the things I said, for all of it. Just make it stop. Make the pain stop! I'll do anything if you just make the pain stop. It burns, Suzy! Please, it—"

The blond let go of his head and let it land like a soft melon on the hard floor.

"Do it for Gerry, Sweetheart. Do it for your brainless friend. Give me the bag and this can all be over. His pain, your pain, all of it. You don't need any of this. You need to go home, rest, sleep it off. You need to make yourself right again, before what's in that bag chews a hole in your heart."

The bag...

Suzy pulled it away from her chest. The blood stained leather felt hard in her fingers.

"That's it." The blond left Gerry, once again moving with a predator's gait. "That's the way. Give me the bag and you can go home. You can start over, get a new job, do something that doesn't make you wear a revolting polka dot apron."

Suzy hesitated, the bag shifting softly beneath her fingers. "I..."

The blond extended her hand. "Give me the bag and everything will be fine. I can put your life back together. I can make it so none of this ever happened."

Suzy stared past her, at the distant trees.

If I can make the forest...

Suzy turned back to the bag, then past it, to the old man whose medicine it had been. She tightened her fingers around the leather, and used her other hand to grab the first thing she could find. It turned out to be a pile of napkins.

The little white squares slipped out of her fingers, hitting the ground like paper from some ticker tape parade, but they didn't stay that way.

They changed.

The tile split and cracked, bright-green shoots springing forth from the fallen napkins and plunging into the earthen grout. They twisted like vines, snaking both out and up, wrapping around booths, legs, and anything they could get their hungry ends around.

What in the—

Suzy's thoughts were cut short by the crack of gunfire and the sharp smoke that followed. She panicked, dropping to the floor and crawling for the exit. Vines laced limbs and snapped bones. More men piled in, only to be sucked up by the hungry green. They screamed and tried to shoot them off, only hurting themselves worse in the process.

Just get to the trees.

Suzy repeated that mantra like some church prayer, her eyes on the exit, the parking lot, and the trees beyond it. The bus stop wasn't far away, but the woods were closer. She could be safe there. She could run. She could kick off those stupid shoes and vanish between the trunks.

She told herself that, and she believed it, but the blonde had other ideas.

The woman snapped out a slender blade. It moved fast and precise, cutting through green shoots and the darkening stalks behind them. It didn't take her long to block the exit.

"Give it up. You can't keep going. It's eating at you already." She sliced through an inquisitive vine. "You can feel it in your bones. Can't you? That's where it starts, but it goes deeper, it will drill holes in your mind." She pointed to Gerry's body, a broken shell of a man smothered in vines and blood. "It takes a heavy toll, to bring them back, to bring all of this back. The more you do it, the more it's going to take from you in return." She stuck her gloved hand out. "I've got a better idea, a much better idea. Why don't you give that to me, and I'll make sure things go better for you? You can't be working here by choice."

"I..." Suzy squeezed the bag to her chest. The heart beneath her ribs pounding like a kick drum. "You killed them! You killed them both! What did they ever do to—"

"That's how life is. The old die and make way for the young. See, I have a feeling you know that." She tilted her head, as if reading the young waitress's face like a travel brochure. "Your grandfather is it?"

Suzy's heart banged against her ribs. "Don't you dare hurt him."

"I won't have to if you give me the bag."

Suzy clutched the leather, the vine's torrid growth slowing around them. "If I give it to you—"

"Yes." The blond lowered her sword. "If you give it to me, I'll make sure he gets whatever he needs. Pills? Booze? I don't know, and frankly, I don't care. I care about what's in that bag. They don't get it." She tilted her head toward her men, all of which appeared to be in various stages of crushed or tied by the born again paper. "They don't understand us. We're different. We can do things they'll never comprehend, not fully. You know that. You know that in your heart. You also know that bag is bad magic. You know it because you can feel it nibbling at your soul."

Suzy nodded slowly, getting her feet under her and trying to come up with a plan. The front door was out of the question. The woman had it completely blocked, and she had a feel-ing the blade could slice through her just as fast as it cut through those vines.

Give her the bag?

The young waitress's eyes fell of the booth, and the dead men laying in it. They'd died for this and whatever it meant. It had to mean something.

What then?

"I can see it in your eyes. That's a bad path you are taking." The blond edged closer, her sword out and shining in the bright light. "You aren't thinking this through. You're getting my good side, the friendly one. I could show you the darker side." She snapped the blade out and let it throw sparks against the back of the nearest booth. "I don't think you'd like that."

Think!

The napkins had sprouted into plants, re-turning to what they'd been. Gerry had come back to life with just a touch.

"...those coyote bones just up and walked around. I'm telling you, Suzy."

Bones.

The trash held chicken carcasses, maybe a few rib bones, but nothing more than that. Would it be enough?

There was only one way to find out.

Suzy raced for the can and the bones inside.

The blond shot past her, the edge of her blade slicing into Suzy's arm and the flat of it sending her reeling.

The bag slipped out of her fingers and onto the floor, where it was hooked with the blade and tossed into the air.

The blond snapped the bag effortlessly out of the air. "This is mine now." She squeezed soft leather in her slender fingers. "Would you like to see real power? How about it? How about you feel that power as it snaps your neck?"

"You said—"

"I lied." The sword woman held the bag high. "Let's see what the spirits think, shall we?"

Bodies shifted. Pale hands pulled at vines, snapping the dying green shoots and pulling their owners upright. Dark eyes and dark faces stared back at her.

The old man was there, and Gerry, all of them pale and hungry, mouths open and faces set like flint.

"This is only the beginning." She pointed the tip of her sword at Suzy. "You'll join them, you know that, right? Once they've snapped your neck, you'll join them. I'll even give you a nice job." She laughed. "Maybe you can bring me my coffee, at least until your fingers start to rot? How does that sound?"

Suzy panicked, her back against the counter and her hands scrambling for something. Her fingers found a stack of forks and knives. She ripped them out and threw them at the advancing men. Most fell harmlessly, but a few stuck, dry wounds refusing to drip beneath the fresh cuts.

"I guess that's a yes?" The sword woman sheathed her blade before turning her attention to the medicine bag. "I tell you what, how about you try to keep that beautiful face of yours nice and smooth? Perhaps don't let them smash it? I'd appreciate it, but whatever works."

She turned away, slipping under the end of the counter without a second thought. Vines rotted at her feet, whatever Suzy had done to them, it had long since lost its power.

"Should have given it to me when I asked." The blonde chuckled, her fingers playing with the leather string at the top of the bag. "If you had, maybe it would have only been one of them breaking you, and not five. I guess it doesn't matter though, not anymore." She shrugged her shoulders. "Kill her."

Dead men closed in, their broken bodies twisted like rag dolls, but somehow still limping, still shuffling forward. There was no passion in their movements, no energy. They moved like automations, like mill machines left to turn. Suzy grabbed whatever she could, a coffee pot, a pan, a stack of plates. She threw them all, shattering porcelain and sending heavy cast iron into the closest face. Bones broke, but they didn't stop. They crawled over the counter, and cut off her only exit.

She screamed and kicked, but they were too strong, and there were too many of them. Pale hands found her neck and squeezed.

Suzy saw stars and the diner darkened. Bloodless faces and dark eyes swirled like stirred coffee, and no matter what she did, they didn't stop.

Drums thundered in her ears, or was it her heart? The diner melted away but for one booth, for the old man who had sat at it.

He was there now, in her head, still silently staring at that black coffee.

When he spoke, his words echoed in her ears, rumbling with the ebbing blood. "Still not interested in the old ways?"

Steam drifted lazily from a coffee cup that Suzy knew didn't exist, but there it was just the same. It sat cradled in a wrinkled and callused hand, clutched as if those fingers might suck the warmth from its smooth handle.

"Am I—"

The old man shook his head. "Not yet. Not in the strictest sense of the word, but you aren't alive just the same."

"I don't—"

He lifted the mug up slowly, pressing it against those thin and tired lips. "I thought you didn't need this? I thought you needed... What was it? Oh yes, something that didn't make you look like a clown? Was that right?"

"Just tell me, please."

He sighed. "You're dead to who you are, to where you came from, to what you can do."

"Can do?" Suzy found herself behind the counter, a rag in her hand and that stupid apron around her waist. "More stories? More riddles. I don't have time for stories and games. I don't have time for any of that."

The old man didn't answer, not immediately, he simply stared out the window and into an empty parking lot. There were no cars, no painted lines, nothing beyond the dense forest, and above it, the stars.

When he finally spoke again, it was with a hint of sadness, a blue note coloring his words. "You are right about that. You don't have time."

Suzy couldn't remember that last time she'd seen the stars, and never like this, never so bright.

"Beautiful, aren't they?" He placed his cup back on the table quietly.

"Is that it?" Suzy tossed the rag and came around the counter, only to find that stupid dish cloth right back in her fingers not a second later. "What about my grandfather? I take care of him. Me. I do that, and now who is going to? My ancestors? They're all dead and gone. Heck, they're probably here."

"They are."

Two words. Two words was all it took to knock Suzy into silence.

She remembered the stories.

Camp of the Ghosts.

Her grandfather had told the tale so many times, it stuck like the burned grease on the fryer in the back. The ghosts were there, the good and the bad, her ancestors. They all wanted to come back, but you couldn't look at them, and you couldn't invite them back.

You could never invite them back.

She hadn't said a thing, but he nodded just the same. "You remember the stories then. That's good. That's a start. They're here, and they know you, they also know what you've done."

Suzy stared at the darkened glass and beyond it, catching the subtle movement between the trees. It was a shifting and frenetic movement, like flashes of shadow against a curtain of indigo night. It didn't fill her with excitement or relief.

It filled her with dread.

"If you remember the story. You remember what you should be doing," he said, just as casually as her grandfather would have.

Suzy looked away from the glass, but didn't close her eyes. "I'm not looking."

"Well, it's a start. They'll come, though. Even now, they're milling about outside. They'll come and if you aren't careful, you'll see them. If you see them—"

"I'll be stuck here forever. Yes, yes. I remember the story. I'm dead, though, so what does it matter?"

The old man waved his fingers over the mug, those wrinkly digits pulling on the steam like a weaver's loom. The blond woman moved in his steam. She moved with purpose and power, each step like a thundering hammer blow. Dark shapes moved around her, not her ancestors, different, deeper, older, and far less human.

Nothing about that woman was human.

"So she wins?" Suzy rolled her eyes. "A white woman wins? Of course, she does. Why wouldn't she? This is their world now."

"Do you want it to be?"

Movement outside the glass drew her attention, but Suzy knew better than to look at it. Still, it intrigued her, like curiosity with the cat, it called to her.

Just one glance...

"No," she snapped, as much to him as to herself and the devilish words between her ears. "No. I don't."

"Well, that's a start." He brushed a hand over the steam, and the powerful woman's visual faded.

"Nice. It's a start. That's great. The nearest I can figure, I'm dead, about to see my ancestors from the Ghost Camp, and my grandfather is lost. All of this, mind you, because of some stupid leather bag."

"You mean this bag?" He reached into his coat pocket and produced the leather pouch, turning it over slowly in his fingers. "What about it?"

Suzy rolled her eyes. "You tell me. I don't know what it is, and frankly, I don't want to know. She has it now and that's that."

He placed it on the table between them. "Do you know what she'll do with it?"

"Well, I don't think she'll make soup, but no. I don't know what she'll—"

The diner melted away like sidewalk chalk in the rain until there was nothing left but the trees and the stars. The trees burned, all of them. Flames leaped from branch to branch, while all around them the dead walked in numbers so great it boggled the mind.

"What is—"

The old man pressed a finger to her lips. "It is what might be, but it doesn't have to be."

They were all there, Gerry, her grandfather, even the other waitresses, but it spread beyond that. There were other faces, faces she'd only seen in passing, faces she knew but didn't have names attached to them.

They were all here, all dead, and all still moving.

Hate filled their eyes, hate, and hopelessness.

"I don't understand. If I'm dead, what can I..." Suzy's words faded on her lips when her body shuffled out of the trees, neck broken and twisted to one side.

A coyote howled in the distance.

"Life and death aren't really that different. You're here now, and you're still there, still on the floor. Can't you feel his fingers against your throat?"

Suzy opened her mouth to speak, but the words caught on something. She could feel them, she could feel those fingers, their icy grip.

"Do you want to live?" She was back in the diner, sitting across from him, a smile on that old man's withered face. "Do you want to live? Or do you want to go with them?" He tilted his head toward the glass and the shadowy shapes outside it, share dared not look at.

Again, she couldn't speak. There was no air to breathe.

"You need to answer quickly."

The door swung open behind her, the friendly jingle of its bell now anything but.

"They're coming for you. They're coming, and they want to know your answer."

Suzy banged on the table, then grabbed on her throat. Were those fingers she felt? "I…" The first word slipped out, and as it did the invisible hand on her neck tightened. "I…"

Shadows spilled over the diner, covering everything but their booth. "We need an answer. Do you want to—"

"Live!" Suzy managed to squeak the word out before the darkness descended, the old man reaching out fingers to grab her own. "Good. Then live, and take back what is yours."

The booth vanished, and she was back on the floor, back beneath that crushing grip, but she didn't see the man for who he was, not the dead and broken thing. She saw beneath that, to the life that roared in his veins. He lived again because *she* willed it, that was *her* bag, it this was her *medicine*.

Invite them back?

Suzy's fingers found his broken face and gently caressed it. "Come back with me."

She wished they'd all come back. She invited them. Suzy didn't care about the rules anymore. The rules were for someone else. The rules were for weak people, for girls with aprons and dish rags.

They weren't for Suzy anymore.

The sword woman had barely reached the door, the bag still firmly in her hand, when Suzy called out for her.

"Give it back."

They were here with her. The shadows of her ancestors slipped in and out of the dark and swinging lights. She was not alone, and she was not weak, not anymore.

The blond drew her sword, bag tight between those slender fingers. "Interesting...I might have misjudged you. It won't happen again."

Sirens echoed from beyond the lot. Someone was coming, the spinning lights splashing the trees in red.

"Give it to me, and maybe I'll keep your face intact."

The woman hesitated, her eyes on the street, then back on the diner. "I don't think so. I think you'll need to take it if you want—"

"Come back. I invite you back. Walk with me."

Her words echoed across the lot and deep into the woods. Her words found ears, dead ears, and they listened.

Coyotes exploded out of the woods, dead coyotes with red eyes and fiery paws. They hit the sword woman hard and fast, taking her down beneath bloody jaws.

In seconds, the blond was little more than a red stain and bits of broken bone.

Suzy scooped up the pouch and pressed it to her chest, laying a hand on the closest coyote's bony head.

The police would come, and others. Men and women would set out to take this from her, but they couldn't.

This was who she was.

She walked with the bones now.

Rail Rider

by Paul J. Howard

Henry Kinkle gazed up at the spray of stars spread out across the midnight sky—motionless dots of white punched into an inky black dome. Below this open window on the wide universe above, the ragged silhouette of pine forest canopy moved quickly past. Henry dangled his feet listlessly over the edge of the open doorway, allowing the rhythmic bounce and jostle of the railcar to swing them out and back with each thump of the track. The clicking and clacking of the steel wheels running across small gaps and imperfections between sections soothed his mind from his otherwise hard-scrabble existence.

Behind him, a coterie of fellow train hoppers lay scattered about, fitfully snoring the night away. His stomach rumbled in protest to the vacancy within and Henry pulled a deep breath against the constant discomfort. He turned and gazed from one shadowy form to the next. He thought of sleep. Better to shut your eyes and skip hours of hunger than obsess on it. Obsess on the next meal, the next honest to goodness real meal. An enormous charred sirloin next to a steaming baked potato. Perhaps, why not, cap the affair off with an oozing slab of apple pie, right out of the oven... Rumble, rumble, rumble. *Jesus,* he thought, pressing a palm against his chatty belly, need a little scratch to take care of this itch. Next town, he'd need to refill his depressingly empty pockets and liberate a little sustenance.

Henry, like most these days, lost much of what little he had when the market crashed a few years back. The world had gone haywire and, though he personally hadn't any direct stake in stocks and bonds and what not, his bosses had. In a few short years, many thousands found themselves without work. In surprisingly short order, his money dried up and, along with it, the patience of his landlord. He found himself on the street.

Ramshackle tent cities popped up on the outskirts of most major cities across the country; the newly homeless gathering in uneasy alliance to share resources and shelter. But Darwin, being the bitch of a fellow that he was, had clearly defined the rule by which these new societies lived: survival of the fittest. The new pecking order had been brutally established. Anything obtained was often ripped away by the next larger man, and on and on it went: food and possessions moving from the weakest to the strongest. Thus, being a rather small man, Henry kept to himself, feeding and sheltering around the edges. Best to lay low, not be seen, blend into the background. Slink through today to survive until tomorrow. Take tomorrow when it arrives and so on...

Eventually Henry, like so many others, turned to riding the rails. Sure, he thought, plenty of danger in freight cars and train yards, but at least the scenery changed as often as you liked. Hop an open car and jump back off when things looked promising.

Henry turned back to the open doorway and again gazed up at the starry sky. The flicker of the tree line below the unmoving pinpricks of light and the gentle sway back and forth of the train's hypnotic cadence pulled gently at his eyelids. The thought occurred to him of moving inside, away from the opening and join his fellow travelers in slumber, but no. He shook himself awake, rolled his aching shoulders, yawned and rubbed his stubbled cheeks. The others with him were complete strangers, joined only by the common experience of having hopped this particular train car at the same moment in time. In just a few years, his battered and beleaguered body bore witness to the hazards of trust. He'd find a quiet nook someplace tomorrow and get some rest.

Henry dropped his attention down to his wrist and the gleaming glass face of the watch fastened there. It hadn't ticked off a single second since a particularly fierce beating he'd taken at one of those tent cities. The timepiece had been a gift from his cantankerous old grandfather and, though nothing fancy, implied value. A small group had demanded the thing and, grievously overmatched, Henry refused. In the ensuing melee, the watch had been broken. In their anger, over the now useless trinket, they'd added a few more licks but left the watch—broken crystal and all—fastened to Henry's bruised arm. Someday, he swore, he'd get it repaired. Until then, he refused to take it off. It did not matter to him whether it got wet during the infrequent bath or more frequent thunder shower, it didn't work anyway. What it was, what it represented, however, was a link to a much happier past and, therefore, a beacon of hope for a much better future. The face glittered gently back at him as he smiled to himself.

A glare flashed across the broken crystal, snapping Henry from his thoughts. He jerked his head up to see something zip across the sky to his right. A sputtering, burning thing that sped quick as a blink below the rise and fall of the moving tree tops. Henry's mouth dropped open as he stared. A few breathless moments later, a faint yellow-orange glow radiated above the forest to the left of where it originally vanished from view.

"Mary, mother of..." Henry stuttered. "You all see..."

Before he could finish the question, feet or hands—he couldn't be sure—slammed his back and he tumbled out of the open rail car doorway. "Toots, ya queenie!", came the voice of the unseen perpetrator as the train sped away without him. Henry tried to ball himself up, squinting hard against the coming uncontrolled landing. The fall went on forever, yet the ground arrived far too soon as body met earth and gravel with enough force to squeeze out every bit of breath inside. Lightning flashes struck behind his closed eyes with each pummel to the head as he rolled and bounced to a stop in the shallow gully that ran parallel to the tracks. Pain throbbed angrily through every inch of Henry's body as he slowly opened his eyes to watch the darkened whir of freight boxes fly by. Tiny bits of dirt and crushed gravel, swept along by the passing train, stung like mad little bees. He rolled face down in the ditch, covered his head and waited.

Eventually, the din of the Union Pacific died off and with it, the abrasive torrent relented. The hiss of flying dust and debris settling back to earth slowly faded to nothing. From nowhere, a distant memory, the sound of receding surf on the Jersey Shore, washed over Henry. He rolled onto his back, gazed up at the glittering spray of stars overhead and sighed. "Son of a bitch!".

With every square inch of him crying foul, Henry pressed himself off the ground. Each flex and bend and movement came with a dull ache and he had to concentrate on remaining upright, once standing. He fought through waves of nausea as his head spun. He clenched his eyes tight and soon the world stopped spinning. He pressed his hands behind his hips, arched his back and let out a long, low groan. He'd be hurting much worse by morning.

He lifted his left wrist close to his face to check the time, a habit he couldn't shake even after his watch had ceased working. The motion revealed nothing more than a skinny, pale arm.

"Shit!" Henry cried out, squinting his eyes, scanning all around for the missing time piece. He scoured the rough ditch up and down the length of tracks as far as he reasoned the watch might have bounced, but to no avail. The old watch, his grandfather's gift and only remaining possession from his prior life was nowhere to be seen. He slumped down to his butt and sighed.

Not one of the good nights, he thought sadly. *What now?*

At that moment, he remembered the flash in the sky. In the ensuing ruckus, he'd nearly forgotten what he'd seen. He pressed himself back to his feet and peered at the horizon line between the tops of the trees and the night sky.

Too low, he thought. He scrabbled up the embankment and stood tiptoed between the rails, craning his neck, peering into the night, looking for signs of the...crash? Was it a crashed airplane? A meteor? Whatever it had been, it fell fast and hit hard just to the northeast. He fixed the direction in his mind and climbed back down the short embankment and settled down against the rise to await daylight. Whatever fell could wait until morning. Henry swept a small spot free of loose rock, pulled his ragged coat tightly around himself and lowered his shoulder to the ground. Tucking his palm under his cheek, he laid his head down and closed his eyes.

CR

The sun crept over the eastern skyline, its light a warm red glow through Henry's closed eyelids. For the moment, the aches and pains from the previous night's adventure had gone missing, like his old watch. Afraid to move, for fear of waking the fresh injuries on nearly every part of his body, he remained still. Slowly, carefully, he opened his eyes. Pain, pulsating and pure, rode in atop the wave of bright light. A sudden roiling in his stomach lurched forward and Henry rolled to the side, doubled up and spewed a hot stream of bile across the black and gray crushed gravel of the rail embankment. He coughed violently once, twice and finally one third time and sucked in a deep breath of clean mountain air, held it. He closed his eyes and waited for the spell to pass. As it finally did, he let out a long sighing breath and climbed hesitantly to his feet. He felt positively swacked.

Telegram to myself, he thought, *try to avoid falling out of trains.* A grim chuckle hitched his shoulders and a sudden spasm of pain exploded across his entire back. "Hi-dee-ho..." he mused and leaned slowly one way, then another, loosening the tightness best he could.

Before setting off into the woods, Henry scrabbled up and down the length of the steeply pitched rail embankment, scanning the entire area one last time in search of the old time piece. After a while, he slumped his shoulders in defeat and gave up. *Well,* he thought, *I guess that's just one less thing to worry about getting rolled for.* And, with that, he aimed himself in the direction of the fallen "thing" and plunged into the thick pine forest.

After a few hours of pushing through the sparse undergrowth, just as he wondered whether he'd estimated the direction correctly, Henry began to smell burnt wood. He stopped and sniffed deeply, slowly turning to gauge its source. He guessed that whatever had come down must have torched the surrounding trees when it exploded and now, the smell would lead him right to it. He pressed on.

Soon, the gentle crack and pop and tick of burning embers accompanied the strengthening smell. The occasional wisp and tendril of white smoke oozed by, light filtering through the trees sparking it like searchlights through a cloudy night sky. Another odor, something oily, mechanical, bitter.

Henry stopped, looked down. There, at his feet, some kind of...metal? A twisted chunk of something that didn't belong. He continued forward. More ragged strips and scraps of something torn terribly asunder. He prodded several with the toe of his shoe. Hard material that looked as if it should be heavier than small quick taps revealed. They didn't sound like chunks of iron or steel either; no *tink* or *clang* when kicked across the forest floor. Just a dull *thunk*. Below each slab of this debris, the pine needles lay charred and smoldering. A tentative tap with his finger though proved odd. Cool to the touch. Whatever these scraps were, they didn't hold heat like steel, however sturdy they appeared.

The further he moved toward the crash site, the more debris littered the ground. Each curled and deformed scrap resting atop charred and smoldering pine needles. Here and there now appeared bits of branches and clumps of discolored boughs and a slow gaze upward confirmed: something came in low and fast, clipping the tops of the trees. Henry looked left and right then paced back to the left, still staring up. Within a few strides, the treetops were untouched. Turning about to the right, keeping his eyes to the clipped tree-tops, he counted paces until the canopy, once again, appeared normal. Fifteen. That meant whatever had come down was around forty feet wide, give or take. Henry knew very little about airplanes. In fact, he'd never even been close to one, let alone flown in one. He guessed that wings could span that far, but the debris...

He leaned down, grimacing against the tightness spreading across his back, and gingerly picked up one of the, now plentiful, chunks. He turned it over carefully in his hand. It was so light, yet looked like a dull steel that should be so much heavier. The edges of the fragment weren't even sharp, like metal ripped from a larger object should be. *Strange,* he thought. He dropped the piece and continued forward.

Before long, the angle of damage to the canopy overhead dramatically sloped downward. With less and less cover overhead, sunlight poured to the forest floor, brighter and brighter with each step forward. Bits of tree became tangles of large limbs and clumps of green everywhere. Pieces and parts of whatever had come down grew in quantity and increased in size. He picked up his pace.

Loping painfully along, driven by the thrill of discovery, visions of hockable valuables dancing through his brain, Henry nearly collided with the thing. It was just suddenly there. Tipped at a cockeyed angle, the massive scale of the enormous disk took his breath away. He slowly backed out from beneath its shadow, taking in the full scope of the object.

The diameter matched the swath of destruction left by the plummet through the forest and after having cleft through one tree after another, each robbing the craft of forward momentum, the battle ended right here. The ship had slammed into this last tree in its path, about twenty feet off the ground, and stopped dead. A bright strip of gnarled wood, gouged by the front end, bore witness to the final slide to the ground, where the nose lay buried several feet below the surface. The rear of the thing had only dropped as far as the distance between the enormous pines allowed and a terrible creaking and cracking bore witness to the weight of the disk pushing against them. For the moment, nature and machine maintained a precarious stalemate.

Huddled around fire barrels, rumors of secret rocket programs, moon bases and even contact with visitors from Mars and Venus spread among the down-trodden. With each wide-eyed addition to the stories, the tales grew ever taller. Henry had even heard talk of government plans to offer work to anyone seeking employment in ever-expanding space colonies—all part of Roosevelt's New Deal. Like ghost stories told around campfires, He took nothing more from them than the entertainment and hope they could provide. Staring up at the belly of the craft in front of him, like something torn from the pages of an H.G. Wells novel, Henry could be sure of nothing.

Slowly, he scanned the entirety of what he could see. From long gashes across the underside, wiring and hoses dangled listlessly. Lining each long strip of damage, curls of hull clung resolutely to the craft. Those curls, from where he stood, looked just like the bits of material strewn about the forest floor. The trees had gutted the ship on its plummet. He could see no purposeful markings on the belly. Henry carefully picked his way around the huge thing, about ten paces beyond the pine, at whose feet the nose lay buried. The large machine really was nothing more than a huge disk. At its edges, it was thin, just a few inches thick, rounded-over, and the whole surface rose towards the center, peaking in a featureless dull gray dome. There were no windows.

No doors. No markings of any kind. If this is ours, he thought, it's meant to be secret.

Holy-moly, he thought, *the pilot! What if he survived?* If this was some kind of top secret Army project and Henry rescued the pilot, he could write his own ticket, couldn't he? There had to be a way inside, but where? He squinted tightly, re-scanning the entire surface. A sudden bright flare of pain shot from the nape of his neck, right over his scalp and clawed viciously into his forehead. He doubled over, palms against his thighs, and sucked in a deep breath, willing a fresh wave of nausea back down into his roiling belly. Between the tumble from the train and not having eaten since the previous morning, Henry felt awful. In a few moments, the worst of it passed and he slid his palms around behind his hips and, with a groan, pressed himself back upright.

He glanced back up to the top of the craft. There must be a way in. Henry cautiously approached the leading edge. The impact had caved in the front end, creating permanent wrinkles deep enough to gain a foothold. Ignoring the smoldering piles of bark and needles trapped beneath, he quickly tapped a finger to the surface. Just like the chunks shed in the crash, the hull was cool to the touch. Henry clamped his palms tightly over one arc of trunk formed ripple and hoisted himself up on the ship.

The angle at which the disk rested was steep, but he managed enough grip to carefully climb the twenty feet up to the domed center. He moved beyond the peak and steadied himself against its backside. Henry pressed his ear to the surface and rapped several times. A dull *thunk* was the only sound it made. He listened intently, but heard nothing from inside. He knocked a few more times... No response. He peered all around his position, ignoring the pain in his head as he strained his eyes looking for signs of a door. Nothing. He swung his gaze up towards the rear end, resting precariously against the two pines. There, probably ten feet away, Henry could see a slight depression. He crawled his way up to it, aware of every creak and groan as the weight of the massive disk pressed against the trees. *Jesus, Mary and Joseph,* he silently prayed, *stay put!*

The spot proved to be a shallow bowl pressed into the surface, no more than an inch deep. Three smaller depressions had been formed in the center of the bowl, creating a triangle of fingertip-sized pocks. Without thinking, Henry pressed three fingertips into them. Before he pulled his hand away, the whole shallow depression lit up in a bright green glow. He recoiled and slid down several feet, eyes fixed on the spot. The glow faded slowly, then after a second's darkness, burst again to life. This cycle repeated several more times until, finally, a whirring sound, more felt than heard, vibrated through the entire hull. He flattened himself down, unsure what would come next, and waited. Several seconds later, after rising maddeningly in pitch, a loud clunk shattered the relative quiet of the forest.

Henry's heart nearly stopped in his chest, his eyes wide, body hugging the skin of the ship. The whirring had ceased and now, for just a moment, nothing but silence. Suddenly, the depression flashed red several times and when the glow remained steady, a hiss of steam formed in a circle around it, rising in a small cloud. The fiery center of this sudden activity slid down and away, back into the bowls of the craft. From the dark hole, the vented steam slowly dissipated.

Henry lifted his head up and tried to see into the newly formed opening. The vanishing white tendrils of vapor revealed nothing but darkness. He pulled himself closer, nearing the rim, and rose up on his hands and knees, yet still the hole revealed nothing.

"Hello?" His voice trembled, unsure what might answer. What if this ship had come from somewhere else? Somewhere not....here? He slowly crept right up to the edge of the...doorway? "Hello?" he reiterated. Only silence answered back. Slipping his fingers over the rim of the opening, Henry craned his head around, taking stock of the craft on which he perched. A sudden realization struck him... *Where are the propellers? The engines? How does this thing fly at all,* he wondered. Rockets? There were none. At least, nothing he could see. Maybe some of the debris ripped off during the crash had been the engines. A certainty washed over him that very moment...

Martians!

Terrified as the thought made him, curiosity tugged Henry on. He slid forward and lowered his face down into the opening. The sunlight filtering down revealed a ladder extending eight short rungs down to a smooth, dark floor.

"Hello?" He called again. The sound of his voice reverberated through the chamber below. No reply. He took a deep breath, slid himself around the hole and slowly lowered one leg over the edge, aiming his toe at the second rung down. When he'd steadied his first foot, he straddled the opening with his palms and slid his second leg down. The distance between rungs was so short, he could easily skip over two at a time. With only a few careful steps, he found himself on the steeply sloped floor, clutching the sides of the ladder tightly.

Henry took in his surroundings. Far from the dark hole it appeared from above, faint light, from no obvious source, allowed him to see the entire space. The inside of the craft appeared to be one big round room. The ceiling rose towards the center, where he assumed the exterior peak of the dome to be, then continued on down to the nose. Even in the dim light, Henry could see piles of debris at the front end of the space. Among the mass of unfamiliar shapes, a single obvious silhouette stood out—the pilot's seat.

Henry loosened his grip on the ladder and slid to his butt. The angle of the floor beneath matched the angle of the whole ship. Moving would be tricky. He decided to explore by sliding downhill, using his feet to slow himself. He scooted to his right and began to inch his way towards the ship's nose. Along each side, from the center dome on back, recessed panels covered in tiny lights gently blinked down at him. Blues and greens, mostly. But, here and there, small patches of them would fade black, then shift to red. After a few seconds, these would fade again to black and finally, return to blue and green. The patterns repeated. He wondered if they indicated damage from the crash or damage that caused the crash. Henry crept forward.

A rumble erupted throughout the entire ship, accompanied by a horrible screeching sound. In a sudden lurch backward, the floor dropped several inches. Henry's heart skipped a beat and he slapped his palms to the ground to steady himself. Just as calm returned, a panel, somewhere behind him, flopped open.

"Jumpin' Jesus!" he cried out and a flurry of small objects skittered and tumbled past. Several slid to a stop against his butt and one came to rest behind his flattened palm. He gripped the item and brought it to his face. It was a block no bigger than his pinkie and, in the softly undulating lights, he guessed it to be a dull gray. The only adornment, a faintly etched set of grooves along one of the long sides. Several more slid slowly by.

Reaching back, he grabbed a few from their perch behind his butt and inspected them. Aside from some variation in the grooves, these were the same. He shook one. Nothing. Precious metals, like gold and silver, were heavy. These were as light as the odd material he'd picked up outside. They reminded Henry of the building blocks he'd had as a kid—worthless. He dropped them to the floor and continued scooting forward.

When he reached the pilot's chair and the debris surrounding it, Henry was surprised to find that the piles were comprised mostly of the same dull blocks. Also surprising... The empty chair. Well, not exactly empty, but certainly lacking a pilot. He gripped the top of the seat and pulled himself to his feet. Here, the ceiling height was no more than four feet and he had to crouch to avoid braining himself of the roof above. He gazed down at the chair. Loose straps were fastened over some rumpled material that hung down over the front and sides. He reached over and gently gripped the fabric, slipping it free of the restraints. It slid through the straps easily and he held it out in front of him.

It was a garment, like a set of coveralls made from dark, tightly woven material. It was small, as if made for a child, but with odd proportions. The legs and sleeves were thin and short, the torso overly large by comparison. Turning it this way and that, Henry could find no zipper nor buttons anywhere. How did you put it on, he wondered.

He let the clothing slip to the floor as he scanned around the chair. There was no sign of the pilot anywhere to be seen. Henry reached over and fiddled with the harness, quickly releasing the center mechanism that held the occupant fast. The two halves slinked over either side of the chair, which he now noticed, appeared perfectly scaled to whatever being fit into the coverall.

Henry pushed his feet through the piles of blocks gathered around the seat, dipped his head to avoid brushing the low ceiling and slipped, first around, and then settled down onto the diminutive chair. He whistled softly to himself as he realized just where he sat. All those stories were true, he thought.

"Martians..." Henry spoke the word quietly, barely above a whisper.

After a moment, the seat beneath him began to gently hum, the vibration barely a hint of warmth moving between the machine and his body. It lasted no more than a few seconds and, when the sensation ebbed, light began to flood the compartment from above. Henry looked up to the ceiling just a few inches above his head and realized he could see the trunk of the huge pine tree rising up into the sky over him. He reached up and touched a finger to the roof. Still there, still solid. It was as if the entire top of the craft had turned to smoky dark glass. A chill ran down his spine. *Amazing,* he thought.

The sudden illumination gave Henry a better look at his surroundings. Surprisingly, there wasn't a whole lot to look at. Glancing down, he saw nothing that would even control the ship. No pedals, no steering wheel, no levers, nothing. He reached down and plucked up one of the small blocks to inspect it in the better light. Again, the little rectangle struck him as nothing more than a toy. The only variation seemed to be the engraved bit along one side. This one, a meaningless squiggle. He dropped it and grabbed another. This one, three jagged strokes. He dropped it and swung to the left and reached down for a third... Another squiggle with a few dots following it.

He dropped the dull gray thing back to the pile to his left and noticed the corner of a case sticking up among the litter. He turned his head and scanned the whole area and noticed several more of the cases throughout the scattered piles of blocks, many half-full of the dull gray rectangles. He grabbed up yet another block. He peered closely, trying to discern the purpose of having so many of these things... They had to be worth something to someone. For the life of him, though, he couldn't imagine anyone giving him money for them.

Great, he thought, what good is a Martian ship if there's nothing he could get out of it? Henry pushed himself up from the chair and, immediately, the whole room darkened. The outline of the huge pine tree vanished, as did the view of the sky above. The roof had reverted back to its original state. Slowly, Henry lowered back onto the seat. Hum and vibration returned, ebbed, and a short second later, the exterior came back into view through the roof, light again flooding the cabin.

Neat trick. Henry sighed. He flipped the block around in his fingers. Maybe he should grab one of the cases and fill it up. They were, after all, alien artifacts. They *had* to be worth something. He leaned over the side of the chair and reached to grab the corner of the buried case when he noticed another item.

He dropped the block and plucked up the new trinket. Turning it over in his hands, it resembled a thick, dark bracelet with a coin-sized ornament affixed to it. The ring of material felt rubbery and soft and slightly warm to the touch. He slipped the first two fingers of each hand into the hole and gently tugged. The material resisted for a moment, then slowly relaxed. The opening expanded easily wide enough to fit over his wrist. He flipped it around and closely inspected the disk-shaped ornament. To his surprise, its face had a faint orange glow. Inviting.

Without thought, Henry slipped it on. The band gently constricted firmly around his wrist and the glow ebbed to a pulsating vivid green. As panic set in, a dull warmth washed up his arm and across his entire body. In one luxurious wave, Henry's every muscle relaxed. He sank deep into the chair, arms flopped to the sides, chin to his chest, and smiled in ecstasy.

A groan of pure satisfaction oozed from Henry's open mouth. Every bump and bruise from his early morning tumble melted away. Pain he'd forgotten he'd learned to ignore, simply vanished. He couldn't remember ever feeling so...

So... Amazing!

He glanced down at the thing on his wrist in astonishment. Slowly, he rotated his arm to get a good glimpse of the miracle and his whole arm flickered in and out of view.

Henry clenched his eyes tight and shook his head. Opening them again, he peered down and there was his arm, just where it should be. He lifted his wrist and brought the bracelet close to his face and, just as it done a few seconds before, his whole arm flickered in and out of existence.

He closed his eyes again and brought his hands together, each set of fingers gripping the other, sliding up and down the opposite arm—confirming—still there. He opened his eyes and leaned back, let himself enjoy the pleasant hum vibrating softly through every molecule. If he didn't know better, Henry might think himself drunk. However, his mind raced along, as alert as ever. This experience was altogether new. His stomach suddenly grumbled.

With newfound energy, Henry slid off the pilot's chair and, as the ceiling darkened and the light grew dim, tugged at the edge of the box to his left. His eyes quickly adjusted the dim space and he scooped blocks into the open case. When full, he swung the small lid down and pressed it closed. An audible *clack* sounded from inside the front edge and he pried vigorously at it. It remained shut. He'd worry about opening it later, whenever the opportunity to sell the contents arose. For now, he really needed to find some food.

He tucked the small case, no larger than his old lunch box, under his arm and scrambled lightly up the sloping floor to the hatchway. Not a single muscle or bone ached or complained. *God,* he thought, *I feel great.* After one last look around, Henry practically leaped up the ladder into the sunlit world above.

An ear-splitting crack rang out into the surrounding forest and the whole back end of the ship dropped a foot. Henry spun on his heel and watched the tips of the two pines propping up the tail end of the disk begin to fall away. He quickly dropped to his butt and let himself slide down the sloped dome. Landing hard at the bottom, he let his knees buckle and rolled forward as the trees finally gave way. The back end of the craft slammed to the ground with a resounding boom and crunch. Birds scattered from the canopy above.

Silence.

Henry leaped to his feet, laughing. He ran his fingers through his wispy hair and stretched his limbs. He felt like a kid. He lifted his wrist to see the bracelet in the full sun and, again, his arm.... flickered. Like it vanished for a split second. He leaned down and placed the case of blocks on the ground and saw that hand flicker as well. What the hell was happening?

He held both hands out in front of him and slowly rotated both. In the light of day, the pulsating green of the bracelet barely stood out, a softly undulating glow in the center of the mottled black and brown band.

Both arms continued to flicker here and gone with each movement. He held them still for a moment. Nothing. He held them longer. Nothing. Slowly, he began to move them and the flicker returned.

Henry grabbed the bracelet and slid it off his wrist. Every ache and pain returned with a vengeance. He doubled over, grimacing against the waves threatening to eject whatever could be found within his empty belly. He slowly pressed his butt forward, stretched his back and stood up. How much of this was yesterday's injuries and how much had he simply learned to bear? He pressed both hands in the air ahead of him and slowly rotated them. Nothing. Held steady. Still solid. Another slow rotation... Nothing.

Henry inspected the bracelet. It really did resemble a watch, aside from its inability to keep time. The soft glow in its face had returned to an orange hue. Staring into the inviting warm light, he hesitated a moment... Did the flicker represent danger? Obviously, this thing wasn't made for humans. What could it do to him? His head throbbed, his back ached, his stomach churned. Did it matter? He slipped it back over his left wrist and the tide of relief flowed quickly across every tiny bit of his being. The dial shifted back to a slowly pulsing green.

He bent easily down, grabbed the case—consciously ignoring the flicker—and loped back through the forest to where his morning had begun. His stomach continued to churn and protest. He really needed to eat something soon.

In less than an hour, Henry tumbled out of the forest to the very spot he'd previously tumbled from the train car. He had barely broken a sweat and still felt great. Amazing, in fact. He scrambled up the embankment and looked down the tracks. He'd been headed west last night. He spun to the east. How far had they traveled from the previous depot? Was it further than the next? He had no idea. He spun back and thought a moment. His stomach cried for action. "West, it is." He hitched up his pants and began walking.

A few miles on, the forest receded from the tracks, replaced by a widening meadow of towering green grasses, waving gently in the warm breeze. In the distance, the shimmer of water glittered in the afternoon sun. As the rail line continued west, the river and tracks neared one another. Eventually, the two ran together, separated by a stone's throw over marshy clumps of cattails. Henry eyed the twinkling water, hunger driving him forward, but the cool refreshing rush of the river begging him stop. His stomach could wait. It disagreed. Henry skipped down the embankment, through the reeds and to the water's edge. He was clearly in charge.

He found a dry spot and placed the case on the ground. He quickly stripped bare, piling his dirty clothing atop the box, and waded out into the rushing stream. He shivered against the frigid water, but it felt great to get all the grime off. Without thought, he flopped backwards, completely submerging. A sudden panic swept him and he leaped to his feet, staring in deep concern at the bracelet. The slow, undulating green glow continued, unabated. He felt no aches or pains. His arm still flickered. In fact, he noticed, his whole body flickered as he moved. Obviously, the water didn't damage it. Still, he thought, better safe than sorry.

Henry returned to shore, and promptly laid against a fallen log to dry in the warm sun. It felt nice. Warm. He closed his eyes and enjoyed the moment.

When he felt dry enough to climb back into his clothing, Henry stretched, rose to his feet, turned and there, no more than a few feet from him, stood a small buck. Its head was raised, sniffing the air. Cautious. Henry could smell the animal, the breeze blowing gently his way. He held still, unsure why the buck didn't react to him. If he tried, he could literally reach out and touch its face. Was it blind? He lifted his hand slowly towards the large head, extending the flickering tip of his finger. The animal was looking right at him, yet, couldn't see him. It knew something was near, continued sniffing the air, but the currents moved the wrong direction.

Henry's extended finger touched the buck's face just below its gleaming black eye. In a flash, the beast thrashed its head the opposite direction, kicked violently into the ground and leaped through the thicket of swamp grass, disappearing in a rustle of reedy green and cattail fluff.

Henry stood frozen for several moments after the deer had vanished. He realized he'd been holding his breath and let it out in a huge whoosh and a rolling laugh. "That was..." he shook his head in astonishment, "that was....odd." He pulled up his undershorts and shook out his pants. With the sun so low on the horizon behind him, the loose legs of his pants cast long flopping shadows in front of him. He stopped a moment, let them dangle. Everything cast long shadows. Everything except him. Where the hell was HIS shadow? He shook the pants vigorously, their dark twin mimicking the action stretched out ahead of him. He turned to face the sun and followed the dark streaks cast by the wavering grasses and trees. Glancing down at his feet, no darkness extended from them.

Henry lifted his wrist and stared at the bracelet. He flickered. It was now emitting a soft blue glow in place of the green. He wondered at the significance. He reluctantly grabbed the thing and slid it off his arm. Predictably, the aches, pains and sick returned. He wretched a tiny spatter of bile in front of his feet, a dark patch within the darkness of a shadow. His shadow. *Well,* he thought, *that answers that.* A slow grin came to his face.

The fire danced against the dark, licking up around the blistering carcass of a small rabbit, hung low over the flames on a makeshift spit. Two ragged tramps huddled near, enjoying the warmth and the promise of a tasty meal. Henry peered in at the scene, stomach rumbling, and luxuriated in the aroma. Time to test the hypothesis AND fill his belly. He quietly set down his box and slipped off his clothes. He gazed down at his naked form and glanced backward into the tangled scrub. Shadows leaped and shrank in response to the fire. He pushed at a branch between himself and the small camp and watched the shadow shift behind him. He swayed first one way, than another. Sure enough, no shadow.

Henry slid between a small break in the scrub and crept closer. The two tramps, locked in low, mumbling conversation, remained unmoved. He couldn't believe it. He continued a slow careful arc around the sputtering fire, stopping opposite the two men and waved his arms. He had to suppress a giggle. Just because they couldn't see him, didn't mean they wouldn't hear him.

Dropping to his haunches, Henry reached out and gently tugged one of the dangling legs of the cooked rabbit. With a small twist, it peeled away from the body. The tramps noticed nothing. Keeping low, with the fire between he and the two men, he devoured the leg. Still, Henry remained undetected. He reached out again and, bracing the spit, twisted the second hind leg from the rabbit. A few gulps later, he dropped the remains to the ground and crept back out of the little camp.

With a happy belly, Henry quietly slipped into his clothing. The two tramps, having discovered the missing limbs, bickered and blamed and dug around the pit. Time to leave.

He grabbed the case of mystery blocks and set off.

CR

Henry woke to the rumble of a passing truck. He stretched and opened his eyes to greet dust motes dancing in sunlight streaming through gaps in the building's siding. It was the longest he'd slept in ages. He glanced at the maroon glow winking back at him from the bracelet. He marveled—still no aches or pains. Yet, he WAS beginning to feel... What... off? He brought his arm closer, with each slight movement, the familiar crackle in and out of view. A subtle vibration, beginning at the spot in which the bracelet clung, had set in sometime last evening and was now moving through his entire body in small buzzing waves. He had begun to wonder if it wasn't related to the shifting hue. Could it be dangerous? He shook off the thought. Memories of each time he'd removed it flooded back. Not only had his various ailments returned, they returned with increasing ferocity, leaving him heaving in agony a little more each time. No, he thought, taking it off would happen *only* when absolutely necessary. Still...the change in color must mean something.

CR

After a few hours of poking about the small town, fully naked and completely unseen, Henry's feet were ragged and torn. Settling down on and upturned crate down a small alley, he inspected the damage. Blood oozed from little cuts and scrapes. No pain. Just the steady ebb and flow of warm buzzing. He'd need to be more careful.

Suddenly, the crate beneath his bottom seemed to collapse and he flopped backward in a wide-eyed huff. Henry scrambled to his feet and, to his astonishment, the crate sat completely intact. He blinked hard several times, confused. He reached his flickering finger out to touch the offender only to have it pass directly through.

"What the hell?" Henry's gaze darted back and forth, realizing he'd spoken aloud. He was alone. He leaned over the crate once more. This time, his finger felt the grain. He gently shoved and the empty container moved. He sighed in relief, pressed down his rising concern.

CR

With his belly full to bursting of hand pie from one shop, an apple from a sidewalk market and a bottle of milk fresh off the back of a delivery truck, Henry returned to his makeshift hideout and dressed. In his tour, aside from the easy pilfering of a satisfying meal, he'd located a pawn broker and determined to see what he could get for the box of blocks. Any price was better than lugging the seemingly useless stuff around. Problem was, he'd need to be seen to do it. He steeled himself and slipped the bracelet from his wrist. Out went the pie, the apple and the milk in a hot, putrid stream. His head throbbed, muscles ached, stomach churned. Hands on his knees, Henry pulled in long deep breaths, waiting for the worst to pass. It didn't. He felt a cold sweat break out on his forehead as he straightened up. Just get it done, he thought, get it done quickly.

Slipping the bracelet into his pocket, Henry grabbed the case with a groan and made his way to the pawn broker. Every step shot pulses of agony from his feet to the top of his head. He continued breathing deep, concentrating on keeping down what little remained of his meal. He kept the box clamped beneath his right arm and his left hand stuffed deep into his pocket, caressing the smooth dial and warm rubbery band. He wanted, so badly, to slip it back on.

Henry arrived at the pawn broker's shop and dropped the box on the counter. Everything itched. Everything ached. He tapped the dull surface of the container with a rapid, impatient urgency. The shopkeeper glanced down at the featureless gray box then gave Henry a slow once-over, appraising the man's tattered appearance. Times were tough and countless people looking just like him passed through the shop every day. Every day another priceless possession hocked for pennies on the dollar. More often than not, the items had been nicked. Desperate times and all. "Yours?" As long as he asked, he could beg ignorance if the coppers came looking.

Henry nodded, kept tapping. "Yeah... Sure." A chill ran through his spine, up his neck and he visibly shivered. "What'll ya gimme for it?"

The man spun the box around, looking for a latch, found none. He peered closely along the seam in the lid, looking for a catch. "What is it?" He pressed several spots and tried to pry the top, but couldn't open it. "What's inside?"

Henry grabbed up the case and shook it vigorously. The blocks inside rattled against one another. "They're like....really fancy...blocks."

"Blocks?" The man leaned back, fists to his hips, and frowned. "Like kiddie toy blocks?"

Henry shook the box again and set it back on the counter hard enough to rattle the rings and watches and pendants on the glass shelves below. "Yeah," he huffed, "Like, rich kid fancy."

The man slowly shook his head. "Look around friend," he indicated the displays filled with jewelry and tools and dishes, "We don't do toys. Nobody buys toys." He glanced to the box, "Least of all blocks, fancy as they may be. Assuming that's what's even in there." He spun the box around again, prying at the lid in various places to no avail. "Hell fire, boy," he thrust out his bottom lip, "Can't even open her up. For all I know, you got nothin' but rocks in there." He stood back from the counter and crossed his arms. "Little box is probably worth more'n the fancy blocks you say are in it," he laughed mockingly, "and it won't even open." The older man motioned to the door, "Sorry fella, ain't worth nothin' here."

Henry, desperate to get something, anything, burst out, "they're Martian blocks," his eyes went wild, hands flapping for emphasis, "Martian case and everything...Got 'em out of a Martian spaceship crashed up in the woods!" He felt his stomach lurch, held it in.

The shopkeeper backed further away, held his palms up between them. *Obviously,* he thought, *the guy's either loopy, drunk, or both.* "I think you should turn around and go." He reached behind him and hefted the baseball bat he kept for just this kind of situation, pointing it toward the door. "Just leave and take that stolen shit with you."

Henry lashed out, shoved the box across the glass. The man leaped aside as the small container flew off the counter and crashed to the floor beside him. Henry groaned, "keep the goddamned thing," spun around and barreled through the door, leaving behind a mystified pawn broker staring down at a worthless, albeit interesting, box of toys.

It was all Henry could do to make the corner of the nearest alley. He shoved his hand in his pocket and squeezed it through the familiar loop. Instantly, warm relief washed across him and he leaned back against the rough brick wall and slid slowly to the ground. After a few long moments, calm returned. He thought of the little blocks. His suspicion had been confirmed. Worthless. Oh well, he'd tried. One less thing to tote around. The real treasure was there on his wrist. He glanced down. The soft magenta glow had changed. It now pulsed a fiery red. It looked angry. It looked like...warning?

"Hey, that's mine!" A tremulous voice echoed through the alley. The sounds of a scuffle bounced through the narrow space. Henry rose to his feet and peered the distance to the other end. A small man cowered against the building to one side while a much larger man loomed over him. They were fighting over some unseen object and it didn't take a genius to figure out who was winning. Henry sympathized with the smaller of the two. He'd been that guy many times over. Still, he thought, not my business.

"Piss off, ya little queenie!", the growling retort of the big man nearly slapped Henry in the face. He saw himself tumbling out of that train car, the same voice echoing down at him as he slammed the ground. Anger boiled up and he found himself loping toward, not away, from the conflict. A wild roar loosed from his mouth as he quickly closed in. At the sound of Henry's awful scream, the big man turned to face the oncoming threat. The bully's eyes widened as the headless apparition rushed onward. "What the..."

Henry lowered his shoulder, closed his eyes and rammed full steam into the big man's side. The two crashed onto the ground in a tangled heap. The bully's original victim scrambled quickly to his feet, out of the alley and to the relative safety of the sidewalk. There, he stared in fascination as the disembodied shoes, pants and shirt leaped up and prepared for another charge.

The large man pushed himself up from the ground and swung around to face the apparition. "What, in the name of Christ, are you?" He balled his fists tight and focused where a head should be. Slowly, the thing flipped its feet forward, one at a time. As each came up in a violent flick, first one shoe, then the other sailed through the air. The bully ducked each as they flew by. "Jesus..." He couldn't understand what he was seeing. A button at a time, the ragged plaid shirt opened to reveal the inside of the back and slid to a heap on the ground. The rope tied around the waist of the pair of still standing pants untied itself, pulled free of the loops and dropped to the side. The bully slowly backed away. Down came the pants, now just a clump of dirty fabric.

"What's the matter, tough guy...Scared?" Henry taunted the big man who now visibly trembled.

"Get the hell away from me!" The big man swung his fists in wild, useless arcs. Henry moved quietly around him, easily avoiding the haphazard fury. "Whatever you are, I'm gonna beat you senseless," he yelled at the pile of clothing.

Henry reared back and threw his palm right at the man and nearly flopped to the ground as his entire body passed quickly through. The man, having felt a brief rush of air, spun round and around, swinging at empty space. Henry stared at this hands in shock. The bracelet's ornament glared back, a pulsating angry red. "Shit," he swore, jumping back to his feet.

The big man turned to the sound and Henry darted behind him and tried again. This time, his palms made full contact, shoving the man stumbling out onto the sidewalk. A small crowd had begun to gather, gawking at the man having some sort of episode, keeping their distance. The bully turned chaotically one way then the other, confused and terrified. Henry slammed him again, pushing him off the curb and onto the street. The onlookers widened, afraid the big man's fits would veer their direction. The man stopped, chest heaving, and stared into the alley. "What devil is this?" he cried out.

Henry lunged out once more, with all the force he could muster, releasing a banshee scream, and gave the big man a push of such ferocity, he flew backwards off his feet right into the path of a delivery truck rumbling by. The startled driver slammed his foot down on the brake too late. The impact rang out sharp and dull and wet all at once followed in a split-second by the dull thump of the bully hitting the pavement, stone dead.

For a brief instant, the world stopped. Then, pandemonium. The driver and small group of onlookers rushed around the still form of the big man and watched a dark pool of blood gather around his lifeless face, the look of terror affixed in death as it had been the moment he'd been struck.

Henry dashed back to the pile of discarded clothing and tried to gather it together. It took several tries, as the material kept falling through his clenched fingers. The bracelet blinked faster, brighter, redder, angrier. His eye caught the truck, still idling right at the point of impact. He managed to lift the pile and jogged to the driver's side of the vehicle. Behind him, at the mouth of the alley, the original victim stared right at him, seeing nothing but a free-floating pile of clothing bouncing into the street. Henry tossed the garments in through the window and grabbed for the door handle. His fingers slipped through it once, twice, then finally, he managed to grip it enough to quietly pull the door open and slink behind the wheel.

Clunking it shut as softly as he could, he looked through the window at the gathering hoard. They were pointing fingers back at the alley, bickering among themselves about what they'd just witnessed. They didn't notice him put the truck in reverse until he rammed down the accelerator. The small crowd leaped to their feet and ogled the empty vehicle as it raced away from them back up the street from where it came. The driver halfheartedly gave chase but quickly stopped, simply watching in shock as his truck raced itself away from the accident scene.

CR

Henry pushed the old Ford as fast as it would go on the narrow, winding road. He thought he'd surely be chased, but thus far, he had the road to himself. He kept the pedal down hard anyway. The highway crested a small rise and bore down into the surrounding pine forest, winding up and down and around the huge trees. The curves tightened and the road narrowed further. The big truck lunged with every corner, forcing him to grip harder. Suddenly, in the midst of a steep right turn, Henry's fingers fell right through the wheel. It quickly spun to the left as the turn continued right. He wildly clawed the air in front of him, grabbed nothing. The truck left road and the last thing Henry saw as the vehicle flew towards the enormous tree rising into the sky... the brightest red flashing he'd ever seen.

CR

Deke Morris pulled his old Ford TT off the edge of the road and peered with concern at the remains of a delivery truck plowed into a tree about a hundred feet into the thick forest. He couldn't tell how long it had been down there. He carefully scrambled down the rough shoulder and approached.

"Hello?" he called out. No answer.

The truck had hit hard, wrapping the front end nearly around the base of the old tree. He looked into the crushed cabin and sighed in relief. Whoever had been driving must have escaped, there was no sign. There also was, thankfully, no blood anywhere inside, even though the damage was extensive. He whistled softly to himself. A soft orange light caught his attention. He dropped down and leaned under the collapsed steering wheel and plucked and odd little bracelet off the floor. It had a soft rubbery band and some sort of glowing decoration. He turned it over in his hand. "Vera'll love this," he smiled to himself and dropped the find into his pocket.

The Ghost Gets Around

by James Stubbs

Douglas Graves, known on his bad days as the vigilante The Gunshade, could count on one hand, hell, one finger, how many times he'd had a woman fall on his car from the sky. Yet, this single extraordinary occurrence was happening to him right now. Her body made an uncomfortable *whump* against the hood of his Ford DeLuxe before his forward speed carried her back into his windscreen.

It cracked but held.

He watched in growing comprehension as the woman frantically scrabbled for and miraculously managed to grip the seam between the glass and the engine cowling to avoid falling off. Her panicked gaze darted his way.

He couldn't mistake those blue eyes and cheekbones anywhere.

Edna Haskell.

He should have known.

In his last adventure as The Gunshade, scourge of the underworld, Graves saved this particular overly snoopy reporter from an almost certain death in a fiery warehouse ambush. To be fair, the ambush had been for him, not her, but she'd blundered into the middle of it, which made it as much her problem as his now.

The powerful flathead V-8 under the hood protested as he let off the accelerator, allowing her to slip unceremoniously to the running board. The pale face that stared back at him almost matched his own, if nowhere near as gaunt.

"Do you normally throw yourself at strange men, Miss Haskell?" he asked, watching as her hands made a white-knuckle death grip on the rear mirror and passenger door.

No biting reply came back. Dear Lord, this was serious.

He'd hoped to provoke some sort of outrage by poking at one of the sore spots he knew she had, her sex and its perception as being weak. He'd known enough women throughout his many lifetimes to know that was about as big a lie as there was but, at this point, it wasn't so much the truth he wanted, but the indignant anger he was looking for.

The Gunshade sighed and slowed to a stop. It looked like Albert Vincelli was going to have to take his chances with Detective Harris and his goon squad. Lucky him. Ordinarily someone as small time as Vincelli, a two-bit confidence man, wouldn't be worth the time nor the bullet, but crime was at a low ebb. After The Gunshade's narrow escape from the warehouse fire, Alfonso Bianchi, the mob boss who'd orchestrated the trap, had gone to ground and nothing Graves had done had managed to flush him or his gang out of hiding. He suspected that he shouldn't expect a Christmas card.

"Get in," he commanded.

She did, without one single ounce of sass at his tone of voice.

The Gunshade kicked the brawny engine of his Ford back into roaring life and took off, using the traffic and the violation of several motoring laws to weave his way through the streets in an effort to confuse any potential tails. Unless Edna had taken to throwing herself out of windows for fun, her article—the one he'd tried to dissuade her to write—had caught up with her as he'd guessed it would. He figured that one of Bianchi's boys was out to tie up any loose ends, Miss Haskell in this case, who might serve as a witness in any future court appearances. Spreading someone across the street from several stories up would do nicely in that regard.

Graves sighed. There was nothing left for him to do other than to take her to one of his safehouses, one that he'd now have to abandon because he didn't have the time to stop and blindfold her and he didn't trust her current shocked state to addle her memory that much. No, the woman had a mind like a damned steel trap.

"They tried to kill me!" Edna suddenly shrieked and he nearly lost control of his car.

"Ah. Good of you to catch up. Welcome back to the land of the living, Ms. Haskell," he remarked dryly.

"Gunshade?"

"Unless you know some other guys who look like me that ain't taking dirt naps?"

"How'd I get here?"

Graves could see her mind racing to catch up with current events. "I was driving, minding my own business, when you made the worst swan dive I've ever seen...right onto my hood."

"He threw me out the window," she said, as if stating it out loud would cement the memory of it in her mind.

"He who?"

Edna shook her head and waved her hands in frustration. "I have no idea. Tall man. Roughly six-one. He had a mask over his nose and mouth. Close cropped black hair and brown eyes. Brown suit, off the rack, probably Woolworth's. Smelled like cheap cologne that should have been musk but was more wet dog.

The Gunshade almost gawked at her but kept his expression neutral. "Nothing about that rings any bells but your observation skills are...not something to be taken lightly."

"Well," she said, not without a touch of bitterness, "when your job is reporting on how people look, you learn. I should've known that phone call was fishy to begin with."

"Phone call?" Gunshade asked, although he had a pretty good idea of how this story was going to go. One of the oldest tricks in the book that wasn't a forbidden apple.

"I got a direct call to my desk. It didn't go through the paper's switchboard. The voice was a woman's. She said she had information on where Alfonso Bianchi was and what he was planning next. I was to meet her in room 22 of the Century Hotel."

Edna paused and shot him a look. "I know what you're going to say but a woman met me at the door. She said her name was Linda and she seemed nervous enough that I believed her story...at least until she shut the door behind us and her gorilla slugged me in the head with his sap and sent me out the window."

"Well, I'm not going to rake you over the coals for trying to do a job that is *not your job*, but, Ms. Haskell, that was an obvious trap. You need to be more careful. You've gotten incredibly lucky so far, so I'm going to stop at the next phone booth and make a call. Then we're going someplace safe to hash all this out. There's probably something useful that you know and you're not thinking clearly right now with all the excitement."

The Gunshade hopped out at the next drug store and darted inside, ignoring the stares and exclamations of the crowd on the sidewalk, but not before handing the horrified reporter one of his revolvers. "Don't hesitate to use that if someone comes at you while I'm inside."

Edna hurriedly thrust the gun into her purse. The last thing she needed was for a patrolman to see a woman sitting in a running car in front of a business holding a gun. Getting arrested for a non-existent hold-up was not on her list of things she wanted to do today.

Graves returned a few minutes later and handed her a napkin with a phone number written on it. "If you're ever in danger or you think you're going into danger, call this number and say the word "albatross" and your location. Someone will come to help." With that said, The Gunshade released the brake and they were off again.

"Is this your number?" she asked.

"Hardly," he replied with a grim laugh. "The last thing you need right now is any deeper association with me. Look where our friendship has gotten you. That's the number for a switchboard that'll dispatch someone from a group that I help occasionally. I can't tell you more than that."

After numerous twists and turns that were designed to shake off anyone following them, but also served to completely confuse Edna as to exactly where they were in the city, they arrived at a rundown storefront that, at one point, had sold hardware. The Gunshade pulled his roadster around to the back and they entered. He flicked on the lights and Edna saw a spartan room with a table, a chair, a cot with a footlocker, and a battered wardrobe. The highlight of the room, however, had to be the powerful shortwave radio set.

"Make yourself comfortable," The Gunshade said. "It isn't much but it serves its purpose. We should have company in a few more minutes."

Edna asked who but the man refused to answer. A knock twenty minutes later made the point moot. She'd find out soon enough. The gaunt gunslinger opened the back door to admit a smartly dressed middle-aged black woman carrying an oversized leather bag.

"Thank you for coming so quickly, Doctor Delva. This is Ms. Edna Haskell, who I called you about."

"A pleasure, ma'am," The doctor said, opening her bag.

Edna whirled on him, her anger rising. "What'd you call a doctor for? I'm perfectly fine!"

"You were thrown out of a second story window onto a moving car—my car, which happened to be speeding at the time. You're probably injured even if you're not feeling it...and, if nothing else, you were, in my opinion, in shock earlier. I think it'd be best for the doc to give you a mild sedative—"

"I don't....OW!" Edna exclaimed and glanced down at the hand pushing the plunger of a hypodermic needle now stuck in her neck.

"You. You..." Edna's legs went wobbly and the woman lowered her patient onto the cot before the reporter's world went black.

Doctor Samantha Delva shot him a reproachful look as she pulled a screen in front of them. "A mild sedative for a thoroughbred perhaps. Was that really necessary?"

"Sam, if you knew the trouble this one likes to get herself in, you'd want her out of action for a few hours too. Thanks for getting here so fast. You AEGIS folk sure are handy to have in a pinch."

Minutes later, Sam's voice called out from behind the barrier, "She's one lucky woman, just some bad bruising, nothin' more serious. And don't you go on thanking me. She gon' be mad when she comes to and you gon' be the one to bear it, not me."

"I'll take the chance. A special agent should be along soon to watch over her and keep her here until I can deal with Bianchi... for good this time."

"Kidnapping and murder," Doctor Delva said with not a small amount of reproach, "If our jobs weren't so dangerous, I'd have some very harsh words for you."

CR

Alfonso Bianchi scowled at the black robed figure standing arrogantly in front of his desk. The silver four-pointed star on the chest of his outlandish attire being the only concession to color. "What is this? Halloween come early already? And why'd you let this clown into my office, Mateo?"

Matteo Berlusconi, his most trusted man, didn't reply but remained stock still, unmoving and staring off into space with a frozen expression of stupid confusion on his face.

The robed man replied instead. "Your man wasn't going to let me in to see you. So I've stopped him for the moment. He doesn't see me and he can't move either. Terrible thing to be such a big man and yet completely powerless. If you can't be a little more welcoming to visitors, I might go a little deeper to his heart. Shame of a way to go in your prime. I'm here to offer you a deal, Bianchi, one I'd recommend you take."

The mob boss leaned back in his chair with a thin smile. He wasn't completely sure of what was going on but the man hadn't drawn a gun and he was still breathing so, for now, it was in his best interest to hear the intruder out. Besides, he was always in the market for deals. It was a language he understood, even if it came wrapped in cheap theatrics. "What makes you think you have anything of value to me?"

"Oh, I have nothing of value for you. My master has only instructed me to tell you to continue to stay out of this...Gunshade's way. We want him. You, and your underlings, stay out of our way and your problem is dealt with. How do you say?...*Permanently*, no strings attached."

"So...I don't lift one finger and you kill him for me?"

"Oh, Mr. Bianchi, your world view is so very small. We need nothing nor want nothing from you, but we are not going to kill him. Our plans for him are much, much worse. However, I assure you, he won't be any trouble for you ever again."

The gangster smiled benevolently. "How can I refuse such a generous offer? He's all yours."

�

Room 22 of the Century Hotel was a complete bust but Mrs. Agnes Nelson, the manager, of said establishment was a veritable font of information. She most certainly did not have anyone currently named Linda as a guest but she did remember Edna after he gave her a description. Agnes hadn't thought much of it at the time because her guests often had friends visit, but, now that she knew what he was after, she gave him a physical description of "Linda": brunette with curly hair, about five-five and wearing a blue floral print dress.

After a five-dollar apology for intruding upon her valuable time, Douglas Graves went into the alleyway next to the Century and it wasn't hard work finding the fire escape that lead right up to the window of number 22. He guessed that "Linda's" goon went up the escape, jimmied the window, and unlocked the door from the inside. Then he only had to wait.

None of this helped him. He could see how it was done but he had nothing to go on, nor any way of matching a name to the woman's likeness. As much as he hated to do it, he would have to call on John Law, namely Detective Harris. He spent most of the drive to the station practicing his most icy indifference to the hostility that awaited him.

The Gunshade ignored the daggers the officers at the precinct shot at his back after he'd walked in and made his way to Harris's office. Oddly enough, none of them dared to do so openly. He hated to intrude upon Harris' domain because he was sure the detective's career was being harmed by their association. He'd have to remember to recommend the man to AEGIS, surely their pay was better than being a civil servant.

Harris looked up from a pile of paperwork. "I really expected you to show up when we busted Vincelli."

"Better you than me, though I'd have saved the taxpayers the cost of his incarceration. Besides, I got sidetracked," The Gunshade quipped, before relaying everything that'd happened to date.

Harris scowled. "That girl is nothing but trouble. You want me to have a word with her boss? Maybe a subtle hint about interfering in police investigations?"

"Well, she hasn't done anything wrong so far other than showing really bad judgment so, no, for now. What I could use though is some help identifying someone."

Harris frowned after listening to the description. "That's not a lot to go on but, if we limit ourselves to known associates of the Bianchi family, there's really only one person your "Linda" could be—Sally Wendell Adams. She's not high up on the list of hardened criminals among that group though."

"I'm not so much interested in bringing her up on charges as I am getting her to talk. Any idea of where she might be found?"

"Well, before they kicked the beehive with you, I'd say the Orange Club. She manages the showgirls there but I can't guarantee that she'll be allowed to be out in public, especially now that they're keeping a low profile. Best of luck...and Gunshade? If you do poke the bear this time, please show some compassion for our poor overworked coroner will ya?"

CR

The robed man sitting cross-legged in a magic circle of gore held a spent .45 cartridge fired by the man he had been tasked to capture between bloody fingers. He took a brief moment to admire the faint flicker of candlelight off of the brass. It was a thing of beauty in an otherwise dingy apartment. The room's former occupant, a down on his luck shoe salesman and drunkard, had paid the grisly price for his last bottle of cheap whiskey. Even among the necromancers of the Silver Star, Ivan Semenov was not a man to be treated lightly, which was one of only several reasons he'd been chosen for this great task for his master.

It was ironic, he thought as he looked at the bullet casing that what had caused one death would now lead to another. This...*Gunshade* was a man so familiar with death that the cartridge felt almost alive in his grasp. The necromancer closed his eyes and chanted an almost intelligible arcane phrase.

There. It was done.

The vigilante was as much now marked for death as those he hunted.

Ivan motioned to the Silver Star soldier who remained impassive through the gruesome ritual at his portable radio set. "Inform the others," he said. "We go now."

CR

Sally Adams was not at The Orange Club, and that was about all Graves got for his trip there. He didn't expect any front that laundered money for the Bianchi family to be forthcoming about their employees, especially not to him, but he'd scared the bouncer enough that he'd believed him. He wondered if an after-hours return trip might be more fruitful.

Graves had just turned onto West Kinzie when he glanced in his rearview mirror, the same black LaSalle sedan that he'd seen for the last four blocks was still behind him. This wasn't completely unusual in Chicago traffic but he'd developed a healthy case of paranoia over the years. He made a few random turns and backtracked two blocks. It was still there. He had often wondered how long it would be before Bianchi got tired of hiding under a rock to seek some payback for their last interaction. He sped up and the following sedan did as well, making their intentions a certainty in his mind.

The first bullet struck the window Edna had cracked, completely blowing it out. Graves didn't wait to find out where the next one would hit as he viciously twisted the steering wheel, the Ford fishtailing with a shriek of tortured rubber onto a side street. He needed to find someplace where he could exit the car. There was no way he could shoot and still maintain control of over 2900 pounds of hurtling steel.

That mass, however, served him well as he burst through a wooden fence and a row of trash cans, into a tenement block. A dog and some kids playing stickball scattered as the sound of splintering wood behind him told him the pursuit vehicle hadn't given up. Graves cursed as the far-too-close *pow pow* of gunfire reached his ears. He was on residential streets and it was obvious his pursuers didn't care about stray bullets. He needed to get out of there.

The suspension of his car screamed in protest as he hit the trolley tracks far too fast, went airborne and came back down with a slam on the other side, barely maintaining control. He heard a metallic *plunk* as a bullet hit somewhere. *Better metal than me,* he thought.

The Gunshade tore through crowded streets, frantically weaving the Ford to avoid other cars and pedestrians. This was too much. He needed to get off the road again and find a less populous area for their inevitable confrontation. He jumped the curb and obliterated another section of fence, launching into an abandoned lot.

It was one indignity too much for the Ford. A geyser of steam erupted from the punctured radiator, and his speed slowed. Graves swore under his breath. He'd hoped to find someplace with cover but that wasn't going to happen. The dead DeLuxe was going to have to suffice. He turned the wheel again, skewing the vehicle lengthwise to give him as much cover as possible and yanking the hand brake to stop.

He rolled from the vehicle and his lone Colt Army revolver cleared leather as he heard car doors slam on the other side of the demolished fence. The Gunshade took stock of his situation. He had cover but they had numbers. On the other hand, he had a clear field of fire.

With a staccato hammering sound the first man stepped through the gaping hole, spraying bullets from a submachine gun in his direction. *But they have more bullets,* he mentally amended as another man stepped through, similarly armed. Douglas Graves found himself missing the simpler days of pistols and rifles, ones where not every two-bit thug had a machine gun.

It only took a glance for him to realize that these were not Bianchi's goons. They had on military-style uniforms but nothing like he'd ever seen before. He snapped off a snot to keep them honest as two more men entered the fray, followed by another man wearing the flowing vestments of an occultist. It wasn't until he saw the iconic four-pointed star emblazoned on the robed man that he realized this was the *Astrum Argentum*, the Silver Star, the group his AEGIS contacts had told him about —and that he was to immediately report if he encountered any evidence of their activity.

Well, too dang late for that now. He'd be sure to let them know if he was still breathing after this.

Lead hammered against his metal shield, preventing him from doing much return fire. The Gunshade set his jaw and prepared to return fire when the two machine-gunners stopped to reload. He saw an opening and fired a shot that hit one of the second group of men. He watched almost in disbelief as the man vaporized, leaving only a crumpled uniform on the ground. This distraction cost him noticing the robed man making strange hand gestures and incantations.

Graves had only a moment's notice of the scent of rotting flesh before he felt something grab him from behind. He instinctively slammed his elbow into whatever it was, thus loosening its hold. In this bought moment he whirled to face the abomination that'd been surely summoned by the man the robes.

The Gunshade hated necromancers even more than machine guns. The bloated corpse lurched forward, remnants of its burial clothes shredded and reeking of death. Graves pressed the barrel of his revolver between the undead thing's hollow eyes and fired, killing it...again.

Ultimately, his tussle with the ghoul cost him his awareness of the Silver Star troops, several of whom tackled him in a rush. He struggled valiantly as until one of them got lucky with the butt of their rifle to his head, and everything went black.

CR

Edna Haskell came slowly back to reality, staring at the ceiling until she could get her bearings and remember where she was. She must have moved because a nearby voice said, "you're safe. Don't worry." Edna opened her eyes to see a young Asian man in a uniform that looked vaguely military but nothing she could place. She did take notice of the winged sword patch on his jacket.

"My name is Kim, Miss Haskell. I'm with...well, a group who helps The Gunshade here and there when our goals align. Sorry about Graves knocking you out but he didn't want to put you in danger and figured that you'd be safer here than out in the streets."

Edna swung her legs and sat up on the side of the cot with a sardonic grimace. "Mister, I have a long history of men thinking they know what's best for me." She spied her purse on a chair and reached for it. "Mind if I smoke?" she asked. "And is Kim a first or last name?"

"No and yes," her guard said with an enigmatic smile.

The reporter sighed. He was going to be one of those enigmas—nothing he said would give anything away that she shouldn't know. Her hand dipped into her purse and, instead of finding her cigarette case, her touch was one of cold metal. Unthinking, she drew out the Colt pistol, realizing that The Gunshade had never taken it back after handing it to her outside the drug store.

Kim's suddenly very serious voice drew her attention back from the gun. "Miss Haskell, put the gun down—now," he commanded, his hand resting on a holster at his hip that she hadn't noticed earlier.

Edna started. "Hold on! The Gunshade gave it to me and I forgot it was in my purse." She dropped the pistol onto the cot beside her, breathing a sigh of relief as Kim removed his hand from his own holster.

Her solace at avoiding being shot was short lived as the gun on the cot began to violently move of its own accord.

CR

Unlike Edna's relatively easy return to consciousness, The Gunshade had no such luxury. He awoke to find himself spread-eagle on a thick wooden platform with his wrists and ankles bound. Darting his eyes to either side, he could see more Silver Star soldiers moving strange looking pieces of some sort of machinery closer to him. That couldn't be good.

He must have made enough movement to draw attention because a moment later the robed man was at his side, looking at him like he was some prized zoo animal.

"You have no idea what an honor this is," the hooded figure said, although his voice hinted otherwise. "It isn't often that one gets to meet a man that straddles life and death...

and you have so, so much death attached to you. You reek of it."

The man fished a spent bullet cartridge out of his robes and mockingly held it in front of The Gunshade's face. "You didn't even make it hard for us to find you, you left your calling card all over the place. With the right amount of blood magic I can attune myself to your own unique signature. I'm frankly disappointed that, given how you make these, you hadn't even considered someone using sympathetic magic against you. So short-sighted, but I shouldn't be surprised at someone with such power squandering it on street ruffians."

Graves looked at the cultist with a disinterested air. "Everyone has their hobbies. Now that you've got me, are you going to keep on questioning my life choices or are we going to get down to brass tacks here?"

"Yes, lets," the man agreed. "After all, there is a certain amount of pride in efficiency. You see, we need souls for our master. World domination isn't easy or cheap. After a recent...*setback*...on an island that you needn't know about, it became painfully obvious that harvesting bodies was, again, inefficient. Mass murder tends to attract unwanted attention, but why should we have to result to such crude efforts?"

"And what makes you think killing me is going to help?"

"Oh, you misunderstand. We don't want you dead. We want you mostly dead, Mister Graves. Or do you prefer 'The Gunshade'? A fine moniker for striking fear into the hearts of common criminals, although slightly pretentious otherwise. We've heard about your rumored ability to cross over into the realm of the dead. We want that door opened wide and held open."

"You're crazy," The Gunshade exclaimed. "You'd unleash the spirits of the dead here?"

"I assure you I am not, and those vengeful specters will not be running amok." The man gestured at the bulky mechanisms around them. "They're going to come through, likely howling for your untimely demise, and we're going to capture them like dirt in a vacuum machine. Can you imagine the untapped power of legions of the damned?

"I won't let you."

Ivan Semenov raised an eyebrow. "You seem to believe that you have a choice in the matter. Now, ordinarily I'd use a knife, but, in your case, we don't want you doing something as careless as bleeding out on us." The man rolled up the sleeves of his robes revealing a pair of heavy brass knuckles on his fist. "In this case, the added suffering will be a bonus. Shall we begin?"

Graves was no stranger to getting hit, having the memories of three generations of gunfighter housed in his soul. As much as he preferred a gun fight, sometimes things got up close and personal and good old-fashioned fisticuffs were the order of the day. However, at least in a back alley brawl, he could dish it out, but, here, he was the proverbial punching bag and Ivan took particular relish in working him over.

As much as it played into the necromancer's hand, Graves knew he needed to stay conscious—if Ivan would even let him pass out. His options were few. He couldn't move his arms or legs, calling out for help was a waste of breath, and his pistols had been stripped from their holsters and lay on a folding table too far away to reach...Wait. There was only one revolver on the table. Had they taken only one of his guns? And to what purpose? No. He knew that wasn't right. Why would they only take one?

Then he remembered.

Edna. He'd forgotten to take his other gun back from her but he couldn't see how that'd help him in any way.

So Graves did the only think he could do—try to block out the pain and think.

Time was of the essence. The Gunshade knew he was tough, but there were limits. No matter how strong his will was, the body would react to the punishment sooner or later. Which, in this case, meant involuntarily going incorporeal. That's what his torturer wanted after all. He needed to make sure that didn't happen.

The thought hit him suddenly. It was incredibly risky, but no more than the dire situation he was in. His captor's comment about sympathetic magic had got his brain working on an idea. If they could find him that way, he might be able to interact with his soul cylinder in the pistol Edna had. After all, who was more in touch with himself than himself?

Graves closed his eyes, ignoring the beating as it slowly continued, stretching his consciousness out into what his mentor, Ghost Singer, called the Great Hunting Grounds. For a place so vast, his astral body shown like a beacon among the drab environs of the spirit realm as he called for it to attend him.

ᏣᎡ

Edna lunged as the pistol gave a small bounce on the taut canvas of the cot and threatened to drop to the floor. The moment her hand closed over the cold steel she could feel him, almost as if they were staring at each other across a busy restaurant. Only in this bizarre situation she could faintly sense his distress and his one overwhelming desire. Edna adjusted his grip and her finger effortlessly curled around the trigger, slowly placing the barrel of the gun against the side of her head. She heard Kim's shout for her to stop as if he were miles away but she knew what needed to be done.

ℭℛ

Douglas Graves could feel his body disengage from the material realm. By all appearances, it was the usual "become incorporeal to scare the gangsters and avoid physical violence" move. The very thing Ivan desired.

He only used the ability in times of dire need, as a way to "shift" out of phase with the material world, unharmed by physical violence. Yet every time he used it, he paid a spiritual price.

This time, his most noteworthy stunt had a purpose other than to prevent him from being shot. He felt a sense of completeness as he made contact with the other shard of his soul, something both familiar and alien to him but there was more, another soul in contact with his second one.

He pushed a bit more. He got the feeling that is was vaguely feminine and he stretched his power out to probe more. Gentle resistance met him, but he persevered and suddenly he was in control of an unfamiliar body.

The Gunshade looked down at hands holding his gun and he raised the barrel to who he assumed was Edna's head. She was going to hate him for this. He needed her in control, rather than him being a puppeteer, but at the same time, he needed to bring his soul fragment closer into contact with her.

Edna, he thought. *I need you to help me. I am held captive. I can get you to me but I need you to trust me.*

Her agreement wasn't verbal but he could feel it. He turned and faced Edna's guard who was looking very distraught at his charge holding a gun to her head.

"Stanley Randolph Kim," Graves spoke but Edna's voice called out. "This is The Gunshade. I am in control of Miss Haskell's body. I am being held by the Silver Star and need to be rescued. I need you to come with me."

Kim took longer than Graves would have liked but eventually agreed. Edna took his hand and The Gunshade stretched out his already depleted soul power to encompass the two bodies before opening a second passage into the realm of the dead and guiding them through.

CR

Ivan Semenov looked up from his captive to see the air across from him begin to undulate and shimmer with a pale light. A pleased smile briefly graced his countenance. "Activate the—"

Before he could complete his command, a man and a woman stepped through the portal and began shooting. They had surprise on their side and two of his men dissipated before they knew what had struck them. But he had more men, men who had been through the fires of battle and were willing to die for their master.

Kim dived for cover behind some shipping crates, but Edna did not. The Gunshade was in the driver's seat and had her fear and uncertainly firmly locked away. Lifetimes of experience and deadly accuracy flowed into her as the headstrong reporter became an instrument of death.

The clatter of return fire appeared as the Silver Star guardsmen rallied a counterattack. MP-18s spat nine-millimeter destruction, but

Kim was behind heavy cover and Edna was a whirling dervish of vengeance, her body twisting and twirling as if it instinctively knew where not to be. All the while, her M1917 barked when it was certain that it had a man dead to rights, it was rarely wrong.

Edna snatched the second pistol from the folding table as she whirled by his shimmering, transparent body. The soul bullet in Edna's gun was the only thing allowing him to stay in the fight so he needed to give her another weapon. It wasn't like he could use it strapped down anyway.

Between Kim and Edna, Silver Star soldiers were mowed down like tall grass in a deadly unrelenting wind.

The necromancer rose up from where he'd been crouched and began to shout strange, alien words. Kim fired and the man dropped, screaming and clutching at his ruined hand. Silver Star men moved to protect the fallen mage, heedless of the fatal price in doing so. Despite the absolute chaos they danced through, The Gunshade and Edna became vaguely aware of the lessening of resistance and spared a glance at the heaps of empty clothing that littered the battlefield. Even in death they fed the insatiable lust for power of the master, The Great Beast. It was as tragic as it was senseless.

It was over in a scant few moments more. Of the necromancer, they found no trace. Kim assured them that he did not suffer the same fate as his soldiers, skilled mages to the Silver Star were too valuable to just be sacrificed. He'd be punished for his failure but they'd see him again.

The Gunshade pulled his influence out of Edna, back into his soul bullet, and then back into his own still-restrained body. He watched her standing still, blinking, trying to make sense out of what had happened. Her dress and mohair jacket sported numerous bullet holes and he had no doubt he'd never hear the end of that. Kim made his way over to undo the manacles binding him.

"Uh-uh! You hold it right there, mister!" Edna said, daring him to free Graves.

Kim and The Gunshade looked at her in disbelief as she fished a battered notepad and pencil out of her ruined coat.

"Nobody is trying to burn you alive or otherwise kill you by...whatever this was," she said. "So you've got time to answer a few questions for our readers...and, for once, you're at my mercy."

Douglas Graves strained at the cuffs and shot Kim a desperate look. "Dear God, Stanley, kill me now."

A Valkyrie in the Desert

by Colin Fisk

The perpetual, thick haze of smoke clustered over the few tables placed close together inside of Harold's club was no bother to me as I quickly made my way through the long, narrow building toward the back.

I gave a short nod to the owner, Harold Smith, who was dealing cards to the only patrons of the club at the moment. Two middle aged gentleman dressed in sweat-stained, wrinkled suits were seated at his table playing twenty-one.

"Good evening, Alyssa," Harold stated as he returned my gesture with a congenial smile.

As he should have. He was well aware that his club's license had been expedited by a local AEGIS representative explicitly on the condition that he keep his ear to the ground and report anything of note to our organization.

I was in a hurry because I was late for my two a.m. meeting with Tandy Hooten at the Dog Club. Cutting through Harold's was the quickest way to get there.

I dodged Harold's brother who was hauling a case of scotch up from the basement and slipped out of the back of the club into the grungy, poorly-lit alley that connected to Center Street. The dry heat of the Reno summer night was a sharp contrast to the humidity of Paris or my own hometown of Boston.

But after settling in over the last five weeks, I was coming around to the idea that I might actually prefer the climate of the high desert. If nothing else, my left arm, which still wasn't at a hundred percent from the combat injury I sustained more than two years previous, hurt less in the heat and dry air.

As I emerged, Tandy was waiting there at the edge of the shadows for me, her eyes darting in all directions as if she expected to be accosted at any moment. She was dressed in a ridiculous looking buckskin dress with garish beading that definitely didn't reflect her tribe's history. A fact she had related to me on more than one occasion after her recruitment into my network of eyes and ears in the town.

"You're late," Tandy snapped as I approached her.

"Sorry. Car trouble," I offered in response.

It also happened to be true. Heidi had been tinkering with the used Model A truck that AEGIS purchased in my name at Calavada Motors. And as was often the case, my partner had gotten lost in her work.

"I've got something for you," the young Paiute woman stated.

I also knew that she needed the money to take care of two younger sisters as well as the fact that she only wore her costume because it was expected as part of her floor show routine at the dance hall and entertainment palace across the street.

"Oh," I tried to reply casually as my heart started to race.

Among the treasure trove of stolen artwork and artifacts that we recovered from the Catacombs in Paris had been a dossier filled with places of interest identified by the occult wing of the Nazis, mostly comprised of ex Silver Star members.

The town and several places surrounding Reno had been mentioned more prominently than any other and Heidi and I had been reassigned to the area to investigate why.

Since time was of the essence, we managed to deadhead on a transport dirigible across the Atlantic before boarding a train that traversed most the United States. And that's how we found ourselves in what was rapidly becoming the divorce capitol of the country only a little more than a week after the battle in the Paris underground.

Naturally, this also provided the perfect cover for the two of us since I was able to claim that I was here, along with my trustworthy confidant, to establish residency and free myself from a horrible marriage. Heidi and settled into a ranch on the outskirts of town and we immediately started to build a network of informants, like Tandy.

"First of all, please don't laugh at what I'm about to tell you. I know it will sound crazy, but hear me out," Tandy began.

There was something in her demeanor that suggested she wasn't quite sold on what she was about to tell me.

"Of course," I replied with a smile, trying to encourage her that I was open to any intelligence she might be able to provide me.

"Fishing year is being disrupted again. And we don't know why."

"Fishing year," I asked curiously. That wasn't a term I was familiar with.

"My people, who you call the Pyramid Lake Paiute, have different seasons that we call years. The fishing season which is happening now, well, the fish aren't plentiful to begin with and those that we do catch are sickly.

The elders are saying that the Water Babies are angry again."

Now, the Water Babies were something that I was acquainted with.

It referred to a creature from any body of water that could grant fortune or wrath depending on how the water and land were being treated. In one of the few books that I'd managed to scrounge from the basement of the British museum prior to our departure, I knew they were primarily a Washo legend. Although it was entirely possible they were part of the local Paiute culture as well.

"I take it this is not related to the Derby Dam that was removed two years ago," I asked since I'd seen a reference to that long standing point of contention in the same text.

The young woman shook her head slowly, her braids bouncing about like tree limbs in a light breeze.

"No. Although much as it had been between the time the dam was constructed and taken down, the fishing season at the terminus of the Truckee River is bad again."

"And the Washo people at Lake Tahoe. Have you talked to them?" I asked, knowing the water at Pyramid Lake originated from Tahoe.

"Our elders have reached out to them. But as of now, they are not talking to us."

"I will check it out," I assured the young woman as I slipped her a five dollar bill. Tandy then turned and hurried across the street toward the building with the gayly-lit façade.

CR

I awoke to sunlight streaming through the curtains in my bedroom and Heidi sitting in a white, rattan chair next to my bedside fiddling with a Tesla stun ray. It kind of looked like she was working on the bell of the weapon although to what end, I wasn't sure.

"It's about time that you woke up," Heidi commented with a smile.

She had been forcing herself to speak only English since we had left Paris in an attempt to cover up her German accent. And when she put her mind to it, she was mostly successful. Now however, was not one of those times.

"What time is it?" I asked even as my eyes were drawn to the mantel clock on the fireplace in my private three-room suite.

"It is half past twelve," Heidi observed as she raised one blonde eyebrow that matched her short cut bob.

"Twelve thirty," I automatically corrected my friend and partner. Heidi was still having some issues adjusting to the American idioms.

"I presume you have news for me," I asked because Heidi was usually tinkering with one item or another in her room by the time I got up. Not sitting patiently at my bedside.

"I do," Heidi replied. "The Patterson ranch had an entire wing cleared out the day before yesterday. Apparently a party of important guests arrived yesterday. Another guest who has been here for more than a month who goes by the name of Matthew Sanders was moved into that wing."

I knew the name but had never met the man. He didn't gamble or seek companionship from any of the reputable—or irreputable— places downtown. In fact, it was that very be- havior that had sparked the gossip mill among some of the dancers at the Dog Club. He dressed and spoke well, had purchased a new Ford truck from Calavada with cash, and he also claimed he was a simple academic. Even though the money he was spending clearly suggested that he had sources of income other than those of a mere professor.

"Do we know anything else about him?"

Heidi tilted her head to one side as she of- ten did when trying to recall something.

"I believe that he had a special interest in Lake Tahoe. Something about a formation north of Zephyr Cove."

"Then why not stay up there?" I shifted up-right.

"That I cannot answer," Heidi replied with a smile. "However, if I wanted to misdirect someone I might not make my residence near the object of my attentions."

"If that were the case, then I should think he would be extremely tight lipped about his intentions."

A slightly misshapen grin spread across Heidi's face that indicated this information had not been freely given. It most likely slipped out in front of someone whom Mr. Sanders did not regard as important.

CR

We pulled to the side of the road and found a clearing to hide our vehicle. Heidi backed the truck into the space and we covered the front with branches. The sweet smells of red-wood trees permeated my nose as Heidi and I stepped out of the truck.

I shouldered my light pack that was popu-lated with a few choice gadgets and tools that Heidi, who always over-prepared for any ex-cursion, had procured from the carpet bag stowed at her feet.

"How far is it to Cave Rock?" I asked my partner as I looked up, trying to gauge the time by the sun's position.

"Maybe an hour's hike. Not long."

☙

As the two of us made our way through the heavily forested area, I couldn't help but notice the contrast in the air between here and Reno. The game trail we were following brought us close to the edge of the lake. Add in the elevation, it meant that the temperatures were twenty degrees cooler and much more humid than the arid heat of the Washoe Valley.

Fortunate timing had brought us to the lunchroom at a nearby hotel as Matthew Sanders and some of his well-dressed guests were seated at a table within earshot and we'd overheard part of their discussion.

"So what did you make of the conversation that we observed at the Zephyr Hotel?"

Heidi gave me a little shrug as she moved into an open grove under the redwood canopy. I took a moment to look up and marveled at the sunlight streaming though the branches as I waited for my partner to answer.

"I think it confirmed we are on the right track. Beyond that, I do not know."

I was inclined to agree. They had been talking about a final shipment as well as the assembly of something. But without context I wasn't sure what to make of it.

We moved out of the copse and as I made my way around the edge of the largest tree at the edge of the circle, I suddenly felt a sharp pressure on my chest. I stopped for a moment and it passed as quickly as it had come upon me. Just ahead, Heidi held up her right hand, her first clenched.

I instinctively froze and listened.

A dead silence had permeated the air. No longer were there the sounds of critters scurrying through the brush ahead of us or in the trees above. Even the light breeze seemed to have stalled into an eerie vacuum.

Then, from somewhere close, I heard a sound that seemed to be rising from the ground and into the air.

Softly at first and then louder, it was like nothing I had ever heard.

There was a low-pitched hum that caused an involuntary shiver to start at the base of my spine and make its way up my back. By the time it arrived at the middle of my neck the sensation felt as if someone had started to stab a thousand pins just beneath the surface of my skin. Every nerve fired at once as the hair on the back of my skull began to rise.

A concussive thump repeated over and over again with the increments between each pulse rapidly shrinking.

Before I could process it all, an impossibly blinding light flared in front of me. Even in the brightness of the mid-afternoon, my eyes were immediately overwhelmed. All I could see was white as the sound grew even louder. The air started to resonate from the bottoms of my feet and up to my knees as if I were suddenly wading in a stream.

My ears popped and then my eyes started to gradually adjust as a stark white sphere shot straight into the air not forty feet in front of me, rocketing faster before disappearing into a tiny glowing ball that seemed to move straight through the atmosphere.

Heidi turned to me, her piercing blue eyes shooting questions that I had no answers to.

I urged my legs forward into the space past the tree and then stopped again.

Before me was a circular depression in the ground. It was as if something very large, heavy and hot had seared its way into the tall sun-dried grass. And just on the other side of it stood a group of men in dark blue overalls and leather aviator helmets with tinted goggles. They were in the process of loading crated items into what looked to be a converted milk truck.

"Hurry up everyone. The next package will be arriving in five minutes," declared a man with a wooden Shannon Arch file held in one hand.

He started to turn toward the three remaining crates which would put him in direct eye contact with me.

I melted back into the edge of the tree and slowly made my way around it so as not to catch anyone's attention.

I turned to Heidi who had stayed behind, feeling felt momentarily dizzy as I silently asked her what our next move was.

Heidi gave me a smile and shifted the well-worn green canvas pack off her shoulders. She unstrapped the main flap and rooted about in the central part of the bag for a moment before pulling out two pairs of goggles.

I quickly reached for the offered eye protection and slipped them first over my head and then onto my eyes as Heidi put hers on so that they dangled from her neck. I still wanted to plan our next move, so I pointed to the opposite end of the grove and stepped in that direction.

Heidi fastened her pack and slung it over her shoulders before joining me at the opposite end of the clearing.

"What do you think?" I asked. "Do we capture them or follow?"

"I think we do not have enough intelligence to take them out now," Heidi suggested, then paused. "But the truck is also more than a thirty-minute hike from here, which changes the equation."

"Teslas then," I replied, determined to try and capture this shipment, whatever it was, as I pulled the weapon from the holster strapped to my thigh.

The decision made, Heidi too loosed her weapon from the cross draw holster just to the left of her breast. We turned back to confront the group when the ground started to vibrate and my ears popped once again.

I instinctively looked up but didn't see anything save for the sun's rays peaking through the treetops. I stared across the grove and there was no sign of an orb either. That had me puzzled, so I flipped the dark lenses of my goggles up and still there was no blinding light this time.

I started to move forward across the grove and once again, just as I made it to the large redwood tree, the sensation of dizziness returned and my eyes were flooded from a flare of white. I quickly slapped the goggles down and I could see, although there was still the sharp circle of an afterimage that slightly marred my vision.

There, in the depression was another ball of light.

With my eye protection down, I could tell that it was about five feet in diameter and that two of the men were presumably reaching into it to manhandle a crate from its innards. There were two more men at the rear of the truck shifting what looked to be a black and tan steamer trunk into the back.

Initially, I couldn't see the fifth man for a moment and then his silhouette revealed that he was seated behind the wheel of the vehicle.

I felt Heidi tap on my shoulder and I turned my head back to her.

"You take the one in the cabin. I'm going to use my new wide beam to try and take out the rest," my partner whispered.

I nodded my agreement, then flipped up the targeting sight, a series of circles, and took aim with my Tesla at the man who I could now see was staring in a wide mirror on the side of the van.

"Hurry up," he urged his companions.

I felt a second tap on my shoulder which was the signal, and I fired. Save for a slight vibration in my wrist, there was no other indication that my weapon had discharged. And yet the man at the wheel slumped in his seat.

I quickly turned to cover my friend but it turned out that my help wasn't necessary. All four men lay in a small pile close to the fallen crate.

Heidi, who had a satisfied look on her face, must have waited until they were all grouped together before firing her weapon.

"Nice shot."

Heidi gave me a sharp nod. Before either of us could suggest a next action, the hatch on the glowing orb slammed down. The crate that was half out of its door exploded in two with a solid crunch and a shower of splintered wood and hay. Thankfully, the spray of flying metal and glass from the transected contents was directed away from us.

The orb started to shimmer and again the terrible hum began. I took a few steps toward it and a knot started to twist in my stomach nearly causing me to retch.

I darted back from the mysterious vehicle, which ascended at a rapid rate, the pain receding with it.

The transport, having shot into the sky at unearthly speed, grabbed my attention until it was mostly out of sight, at which point my eyes were drawn to the four figures that Heidi had stunned. Each man now looked like a large rock had been dropped on them. Blood leaked from their eyes, ears and the tips of their fingers, as well as pooling around their lower abdomens and feet. There was no doubt in my mind that they were dead, most likely due to their proximity to the orb's takeoff.

"Ugh," Heidi commented as she too took in the sight in front of us.

"Agreed," I replied as my mind started to race.

While part of me wanted to do the right thing and give these men a proper burial, I also had no idea if another one of those orbs was coming soon. And given what had happened to the unconscious men, I also knew that I did not want to be in its proximity if it landed.

"I know it's not right, but we should tie up the survivor and utilize the truck to take him and his cargo back to Reno. We can pick up our own vehicle on the way and then examine what we've found."

"I understand," Heidi replied as she paused to make the sign of the cross over each body, while I proceeded to restrain our prisoner before he woke up.

ॐ

I made a quick detour to the local AEGIS office, which was in the basement of the Woolworth's building, to drop our still unconscious prisoner off for questioning. Then I drove our Model A to an out of the way, prearranged rendezvous spot. A clearing near the California border where Heidi was waiting for me with the captured milk truck.

A quick check of the truck's contents did not tell us much. Three crates as well as the steamer trunk were held in place by clearly pre-fitted borders comprised of two-by-fours that had been nailed into position so that their contents would not shift during transit.

The single remaining open space looked approximately the size of the destroyed crate.

If there were preset slots for their cargo it meant there wasn't a third shipment and I felt a small pang of guilt in not burying the men in the forest.

Since the trunk was the easiest to access, Heidi reached in and hauled it out. Rather than picking the lock, she drew her hunting knife and cut across the leather straps that held the lid in place.

What we found was certainly nothing like I had guessed. The upper tray held a starched gray uniform with a black collar. On the left-hand collar was the stylized SS of the German Waffen.

I lifted the tray out and beneath were another three uniforms as well as hats to complete the ensembles.

"*Verfluchte schweinerie*," burst out of Heidi's mouth.

I wasn't familiar with the words, save for part of the second meaning, *pig*, but it was clear from the disgust in her voice that this was not a term of endearment.

"I won't ask what that means."

I knew darn well just how much Heidi hated the Nazis that had started to take over her homeland. Just as I also had no doubt that she was cursing their very existence.

I dropped the tray back in and closed the lid, shoving the trunk down the center aisle of the vehicle as I pulled a claw hammer from the toolbox conveniently stashed in its own spot in the truck.

"Let me," Heidi insisted as she hopped up inside the cargo area.

I realized that the temperature of the vehicle was a little warmer than the heat of the day. Either our captors weren't planning on using the refrigerated storage or what little ice they had brought was melted.

There was a loud screech of rending wood and nails and Heidi tossed the hammer aside before reaching into the crate. I heard a rattling sound as Heidi pulled out an ammo belt with some very large bullets. It was the type that fed into the machine gun of a plane or maybe a vehicle mounted weapon.

"Well, that's certainly not a good thing," I muttered.

A quick check of the other crates revealed two more filled with belts of ammunition. The longer, skinny one held the machine gun they clearly belonged to.

The final crate was roughly eighteen inches square and contained a bronze-hued orb that was polished so brightly that it seemed to reflect everything in sight.

My hand was inexplicably drawn to it. When my fingertip made contact with the surface, to my surprise, it rippled and my finger was enveloped by warmth as I pressed into what seemed like cool liquid metal. I withdrew my digit quickly and examined it. I couldn't explain the reason, but it was completely dry.

Heidi looked completely nonplussed. She too poked at the orb with her finger and stared at her own digit after she pulled it back.

"What on Earth is this?" she asked.

"Maybe the packet of papers on the clipboard will give us some more information," I suggested, since that seemed to be the only source of official paperwork in the vehicle.

CR

"Are you certain that we are in the right area," Heidi asked as we bumped our way along the farm road outside of Fallon.

"I am."

"We should be seeing the barn soon," Heidi insisted as she stared at the detailed map that we'd found among the papers in the milk truck. "We have to be practically right on top of it."

I searched the empty flat space ahead of me and still saw no structure in sight. I felt sick to my stomach for a moment and then suddenly we were at the edge of a field full of dried, tan grass and there, not half a mile away, was an oversized barn. The wooden walls were sloughing sun-bleached red paint like a bad sunburn. At the peak of the barn's crest sat the rounded shape of the stealth dirigible that the plans had detailed.

I stomped on the truck's brakes and assessed the what had just happened.

To my left was a generator with two leads trailing off into a fifty-foot-wide pond with reflective brass sheen and several dead fish along the edges. Suddenly everything made sense to me.

Apparently, Heidi had figured it out as well because she shot a knowing look in my direction.

"The material," she gasped. "You add an electrical current to it which generates a reflective field that effectively renders an area invisible, until you pass through the curtain, for lack of a better term."

"That explains why we couldn't see the orbs until after we were around the tree," I replied.

"Exactly. But I wonder. Yes," Heidi threw me a smile that she got when she was struck by a sudden insight. "I am willing to bet that you can mold the field such that you could create a cylinder that would allow the orbs to transport relatively unseen. Just as this small body of water can most likely obfuscate a large area, I am certain that if it were contained in something to allow it to project upward that the orb would only be visible momentarily at the speeds it was traveling."

"That makes sense," I agreed as I gazed toward the barn. There appeared to be movement at the open doors, and I wondered for a second if we'd been spotted.

The sharp crack of a rifle being fired in our direction followed quickly by the whistle of the round passing the truck's open window answered my question.

I shifted the truck into gear and slammed the accelerator pedal to the floor as Heidi started to frantically dig into the carpetbag filled with weapons and useful items that she had restocked while back at the ranch.

The smart thing would have been to turn right around and retrieve the orb from where we had hidden it in the woods near the border, but all my instincts told me that we didn't have the time. Any secrecy about our visit was now out the door. I turned the truck into the grass field, feeling the back wheels drift out for a moment, which was what I was hoping for.

I reasoned that the tall grass would provide us some cover and if the back end would randomly slip out then it would also make it harder for them to target us.

A bullet blasted through the windshield not six inches from my ear.

Heidi popped up, a familiar Thompson submachine gun in her hands. She propped it out the open window and started to fire.

I could hear the familiar sound of high pitched turbines starting to rotate and a massive dust cloud started to erupt from the open barn doors, effectively blinding our attackers.

The airship's props had clearly spun up and they were going to try and escape in the dirigible.

"Not on my watch," is what erupted through my brain as I floored the truck, trying to get close enough to prevent the launch of this new aircraft.

We covered the half mile distance in less time than I would have expected, the truck bouncing and jostling as the tires transitioned from the grass to the dirt patch in front of the barn. I slammed on the brakes and hauled over hard on the wheel, skidding to a stop.

The truck came to a rest and Heidi reached between her legs and handed me a drum-fed shotgun before she opened the door, her goggles down to protect her eyes from the propeller wash.

I settled my own eye protection into place before I slammed open the door and paused behind it, not wanting to expose myself too much. It turned out to be a wise decision, as small arms fire started to pepper the door. Given that the shots didn't penetrate the metal, I was guessing that the attacker had switched to a pistol of some sort.

Taking a quick glance above the truck door, I spotted the gunman hiding behind a stack of wooden crates just to the left of the barn's threshold.

The pitch of the airship's turbines rapidly increased and it was apparent to me they had now come up to power. The angle of the wash also changed as the craft clearly started to ascend.

I braced the shotgun against my shoulder and top of where the window met the door and stood up, centering my weapon on the crates. The gunman, who I could now see was wearing black overalls, stepped out. I fired, hitting him center-mass and causing him to fly back behind the stacks.

Heidi moved into the field of my vision, sprinting toward the open door and yelling at me that they had only left one person behind to slow us down.

I abandoned my shotgun and raced toward the barn, trying to catch up with my partner.

We got into the building just as the dirigible cleared the top of the barn. The cable that had been used to tie the airship down was dragging through the dirt and hay floor as it rose with the craft.

I leaped forward and tried to grab a hold of it.

My hands grasped around the one-inch hemp for a moment. And then my injured left hand spasmed, causing me to lose my grip.

I watched helplessly from the ground as the line rapidly rose into the air, now out of reach.

I could see the wide grins of the two pilots, also dressed in black overalls, staring down at us through the glass of the cockpit. I recognized them both from yesterday's lunch at Zephyr Cove.

"Alyssa, hurry," Heidi called out, pointing to the right-hand wall.

My eyes followed her finger and there, in the nearest stall, was a dressmaker's mannequin with a jetpack, its harness draped over the shoulders of the frame.

Even though I hadn't been in the air since Romania, I knew it was our only chance to catch the airship now.

I pushed off the ground and stood up, following Heidi who had already lifted the double jetted pack off the dummy. I quickly made my way over, turning at the last moment so that Heidi could help strap me in.

It may have been more than two years since I was wounded, but the familiar weight that draped over my shoulders was like coming home. I started adjusting the front straps and bucking myself up appropriately. I familiarized myself with the controls as everything started to come back to me like second nature.

While I had never flown a Silver Star or Nazi jetpack, the principals were the same as the AEGIS packs. There was a grip-based locking throttle on the right handle and a wrist controlled rudder tied to the left. The power switch was just under the right armpit and I instinctively triggered it, the electric battery humming to life.

As the straps cut slightly into my trapezius muscles, I took a deep breath. Heidi gave me a slap on the gyro housing and I moved forward toward the barn doors. I didn't want to shoot directly up because I was worried that I would impact with the slower moving dirigible.

Each heavy step I took brought back great memories of climbing the stairs on any number of AEGIS craft. My sisters and myself ready to get up to the rim of the basket to fight in the air. I couldn't help but smile as I walked into the light and depressed the throttle.

There was the familiar tug as I was propelled upward. My heart started to race as my feet left the ground. I rocketed into the air, away from the barn, before I used the rudder to swing myself around to get my first look at the craft in front of me. It had swung around and was now moving away from the barn toward the southwest.

An exhilaration coursed through my veins that I hadn't realized I'd been missing. The wind whipping through my hair, the slight chill as I ascended in altitude. There was something so pure and right about it.

All I wanted to do was keep flying, but I had a mission to accomplish, and that took precedence.

I knew from the captured plans this was much smaller than a craft like the *Daedalus* class light recon airships. But I was still surprised at its compact nature. While the *Daedalus* herself was about two-hundred-fifty feet in length, this ship had to be a third of the size, which made a sort of sense. If they had the stealth material installed then you would want as compact a footprint as possible so as not to utilize too much of your power to cloak your vessel.

Suddenly the noise in the air changed. Where previously there had been the high pitched whine of the airship's turbines, now all I that I could hear over my own pack's motor was the sound of air being compressed by the turbofans.

So, in addition to the reflective material, apparently there was a whisper mode to allow the craft to approach a target silently.

It wasn't going to help them because I had them in my sights and I was rapidly approaching from their blind spot.

As I swung around to the left side of the cockpit, I pulled my Tesla pistol from its place in my now unsnapped thigh holster. A flick of the wrist and the sights were up.

The looks on the two men in the cockpit were priceless as I swung into view and fired twice, knocking both of them unconscious.

Then it was a simple matter of gliding to a landing on the gantry above the cockpit. There was a convenient door, not even a hatch, and I was inside, pack and all.

I made my way down the stairs and into the cockpit. The radio on my left hip crackled to life and Heidi's voice was coming through loud and clear.

"What do we do now?" she asked.

"First, I will secure my prisoners. And then I will figure out how to fly this bird. After all, I'm pretty sure that a ship like this as well as the stealth material will throw the boffins down at Moffett Field into a tizzy."

"I approve," Heidi's voice called through the radio. "While you are filling out the paperwork, I will head back up to the lake to acquire the cloaking device near the landing spot. We can meet at the clearing near the border, grab the other orb, and then you and I can take a little flight to drop them off."

"That sounds perfect," I replied as I pulled a pair of handcuffs from the left thigh pocket of my trousers.

This should help resolve the Pyramid Lake fishing issue, I thought as I felt the wind calling me to play in its currents.

As Above, So Below

by Rose Lamont

It was a strange case, to be sure.

Serial murders were one thing. Creepy, but bearable. Cult suicides? Not only were they weird, but they required much more research than Sid Cooper, ace detective with the homicide department, was willing to do on any given day. So, as the manila folder landed on his desk and he skimmed through it (victims' eyes were all melted out of their skulls—disgusting), he stifled a shudder and asked, "Why me?"

"Chief says this is for arresting the wrong guy last time," his associate who had made the delivery answered, "Says if you do good this time, he might let you keep your job."

Keeping his job was something that Sid definitely wanted to do, so he made contact with the mother of one of the victims.

"I just don't know how it could have happened," she cried. "I don't know what was so unfulfilling about his life that he would go and join a *cult*."

"Were there any signs that you noticed when he first started?" Sid asked.

"No, not that I can..." the old woman began, before hesitating. "...well..."

"Please, anything you know could help."

"He did start wearing this necklace." She fished something out of the pocket of her dressing gown and held it out for Sid to look at. It was indeed a necklace, adorned with plastic beads and a quaint little sparkly blue butterfly, akin to something that a six-year-old girl would wear, rather than a man in his mid-thirties.

Sid quickly slipped on a pair of leather gloves from his coat pocket and held out his hand. "May I?"

The old woman dropped the necklace into his outstretched hand without question. "Of course. It's a strange thing, isn't it? They found it still around his neck during the autopsy. He literally wore it until the moment he died. I can't imagine why it would be so special to him."

Sid moved the necklace around in his hand as the woman kept rambling and he stopped listening. She was right, though; what could possibly be so important about a plastic kids' toy necklace that a grown man would wear it to his supposedly planned death?

He glanced back up at the woman. "Anything else?"

She looked somewhat surprised, but she said, "Well... Yes, actually, let me see if I can find it."

She got up from her chair and left the room for a moment before coming back with a leather-bound book, stuffed with pieces of ripped-out notebook paper. "He would study this all the time," she said, handing it to Sid.

"Ah... thank you," he said, taking the book and getting up from his chair as well, "Mind if I take these back to the station? I think they will prove to be valuable evidence."

"Of course, whatever you need," the old woman said.

Sid said his politest goodbyes and was gone, back to the station. It was late, however, and nobody of importance was there—nobody who could help him look through this damned book. Sid Cooper was lazy, but he was also impatient. He wanted answers now. So he went to his office, sat at his desk, and opened the book.

The original pages were filled with sigils and words in a language that Sid was unfamiliar with. Luckily, however, the notebook pages that were stuffed inside seemed to be translations. They were instructions, for some kind of ritual. He did a cursory flip through the rest of the pages and found that they all were extremely similar. Draw this sigil. Wear this amulet. Amulet, amulet, amulet. They all mentioned the amulet. Well, Sid didn't have an amulet.

But he *did* have...

He pulled the necklace out of his pocket and eyed it for a moment, before sighing and hanging it around his neck. He figured he might as well try one of these rituals. No research like hands-on research.

"Draw sigil on floor as it appears on page," he read aloud. He looked at the sigil displayed on the original page of the book and sighed again. Why did he have to randomly pick one that was so complicated?

He picked up a piece of chalk from his wheeled chalkboard and pushed around some furniture to make room on the floor. "Here goes nothing," he mumbled as he got to work. This circle here, then a line from here to there...

He did his absolute best to recreate the design, wondering to himself multiple times why he was trying so hard, but deciding he had nothing better to do on a Tuesday night.

Then he stood on one side of the intricate circle he just drew, and chanted. Well, he did his best, anyway. He stumbled on a few words, not really knowing how to pronounce the random apostrophes. And when he was done...

Nothing. It was quiet in his office, just as it had been before. Of course nothing happened; Sid didn't believe in any of that occult hooey anyway.

He turned to slink dejectedly back to his chair, when he noticed someone—or something—there already. Something with horns. Big, curly horns, like those of a ram. Whatever it was was huge, just barely able to fit in the chair at all, and, although it appeared dark, as though surrounded by a black mist such that most of the grisly details of its features were hidden from clear sight, Sid could make out glowing red eyes and a mouth full of sharp, pointed teeth arranged in a smarmy grin. The teeth didn't move, but Sid heard a deep, growling voice come from somewhere in the back of his mind, ringing across the confines of his skull in an echo that sent chills down his spine: "You called?"

Sid stared, dumbfounded, not knowing in the slightest how to respond. Every logical part of him was looking at this...thing, and completely giving up hope as to finding any reasonable explanation for any of this. "I-I-I did?" he stammered.

The creature grinned wider and stood slowly, impressively revealing every inch he had on Sid, which happened to be many, many inches. At least a foot. It reached a clawed hand out, darkness swirling around it. "You have my amulet."

Sid instinctively touched the tiny plastic butterfly that was hanging around his neck. "A-amulet? You mean this thing?"

The creature beckoned with its claws to hand it over. "I would like it back."

Every part of Sid wanted to give the creature what it wanted so that it could go back to wherever it came from and he could go back to his normal life. Except one part. One tiny part that adamantly refused to give the creature anything out of spite. And that part clutched the butterfly, holding onto it for dear life. "I-I —" he began.

Before he could stutter anything vaguely resembling words, his office door swung open, revealing a woman he recognized but didn't see very often. "Hey there, Sid, whatcha—"

And before *she* could finish her thought, a clawed hand veiled in inky darkness shot out, and with the sound of a loud, visceral crack, Ada's eyes rolled back in her head and she collapsed onto the floor before them.

Sid looked at the limp body on the floor and then back at the creature, whose grin was gone. "What'd you do that for?!" Sid exclaimed, his tone hushed, in case anyone was still around.

"I'm sorry," the creature's voice resounded, "She startled me. I didn't mean to."

"*Startled* you? Startled *you*? Is...is she dead?!" Sid rushed to the body to examine it, checking for any sign of breathing or a pulse. Nothing. He couldn't even find any obvious causes of death. "What did you *do* to her?"

"Disconnected the brain stem from the spinal cord."

"...*Why?*"

"I don't know, she startled me!"

Sid sighed, pinching the bridge of his nose. "This is bad. This is *really* bad."

"It's not *all* bad," the creature's voice reverberated across Sid's brain, exacerbating the headache that had begun to form. "It was just another measly human."

"No. No," Sid disagreed, looking the eldritch terror directly in its godawful face, "She was not just another measly human, she was the *Chief's secretary*. Somebody who is going to be sorely missed. Plus, I think she had a husband at home..."

Sid's mind started running at a million miles an hour as he tried to figure out what in the hell he was ever going to do about the situation at hand, until the demonic voice in his head began humming some kind of wistful tune, and somewhere behind him, he sensed movement. Behind him, where the body was...

He turned around. There was Ada's body, up and moving around, dancing all by itself as the swirling darkness oozed out of every visible orifice.

"Wh—what are you doing?"

"Dancing!" The voice in Sid's head sounded at the same time the woman's voice (or, at least, an approximation thereof) came out of the body's mouth.

"Would you stop? I'm trying to... Wait a minute..." Sid suddenly got an idea. A horrible, selfish, morbid idea, but an idea nonetheless, which is more than he usually had. "If it wasn't for that...darkness...fog...thing, this might actually be great."

"What, the miasma?" the voice clarified. "Only you can see that. Just like you're the only one that can see me."

"Really?" Sid's lips spread into a conniving grin. "Then this is *definitely* going to work out. How long can you do that for?"

"As long as I want," the creature's voice lingered in Sid's ears along with the warbled voice of the woman's body. "At least... until the body rots."

"That shouldn't be for a while though, right?" Sid said more to himself than to anyone else. "This'll be fine. Everything will be fine. It'll give me time to think of a way to deal with this... and then everything will be fine!"

"Everything will be fine..." the voice sang as the body continued dancing.

"We are definitely going to have to go over some things, though, like...talking."

"Talking?" The body stopped dancing and faced Sid with its arms at its side in an almost puppet-like fashion. "What's wrong with the way I talk?"

"Well...just try not to talk for extended periods of time. We'll say you have a cold and that's why your voice is all...croaky like that." Sid considered the way the body was currently standing as well. "And don't ever just stand like that, it's creepy."

"What am I supposed to do instead?"

"I don't know, move your arms or your head or something."

The body's arms flopped around like dead fish.

Sid sighed in exasperation. "No, I mean... put them on your hips or something, like women do."

The body did as was suggested, and instantly looked ten times more human, like it was going to nag him for not doing the dishes or something. "That's better," Sid said.

"Now," he continued, "The Chief is coming in in a few hours. You are his secretary, so you're supposed to do what he says. Only answer him with 'Yes, Chief.' We don't want to give away the fact that you're actually a dead body being puppeteered by a...what are you again?"

"I am Killgrath, Archduke of the Underworld."

"...Right. That. Now, let me show you how to use a typewriter."

As it turned out, using a typewriter was incredibly difficult when fine motor skills were less than existent. Possessing a body really was like using a puppet; it was pretty easy to make it *look* like it was using a typewriter, but actually producing anything from the performative action of moving the hands around the keyboard was nigh impossible. Nevertheless, the detective and the demon worked together throughout the rest of the night, learning how menial office tasks were done. Many times, Killgrath complained, although he could readily admit it was fascinating how humans could have anything at all going on for them that would require them to do these things.

The next day, after a full night of instruction, Sid retreated back to his office to sit in his chair and rest his eyes. Killgrath (aka Ada the Chief's secretary), who thought himself fully prepared, sat at the now-dead woman's desk, pretended to type as he was taught, and waited.

Promptly at 7:00 AM, the Chief, all six feet of pure masculinity, strode past Ada's desk with a, "Morning, Ada. Were you here all night?"

Killgrath responded with the only thing he had been permitted by Sid to say: "Yes, Chief."

The Chief slowed on his way to his own office, giving Ada a suspicious look. "You sick or something? You look pale."

"Yes Chief." Killgrath forced a smile onto the body's face, which did not lessen the Chief's suspicion whatsoever.

"I don't want you pulling all-nighters if you're sick, Ada. I appreciate you being here, but you don't need to kill yourself for the department." The Chief offered a short, ironic laugh.

Killgrath responded with a laugh of his own, which came out of the body as more of a rapid, heaving, loud series of breaths. Apparently laughing in a borrowed body was also extremely difficult.

All previous evidence of mirth faded quickly from the Chief's face. "Are you sure you're feeling alright?"

"Yes, Chief."

The Chief hesitated, giving the body of his secretary another look-over, before finally saying, "You should go home. Rest up. Be at your best tomorrow. I'll have Cooper do my dictation today." He laughed again.

Killgrath decided against laughing with him this time. "Yes, Chief."

Still laughing, the Chief entered his office and closed the door behind him.

Killgrath got up from Ada's desk and walked the body into Sid's office, making sure his door was also closed before releasing the body, which collapsed to the floor with a thud.

The sudden noise woke Sid, who opened his eyes to a familiar sight—the Chief's secretary in a crumpled heap on the floor, and a monstrous creature towering over him.

"What the hell are you doing?!" Sid exclaimed, launching himself out of his chair toward the body.

"The Chief said to go home," Killgrath's voice resounded inside Sid's head. "I didn't know where that was, so I came here."

"Well, you can't just leave her on the floor like that," Sid said, lifting the body from under the arms. The first place he thought of to put the body was into the chair in which he was previously sitting. "I don't know why I'm doing this myself when you could just move the body with your mystical demon powers."

"It's funny to watch you suffer," the voice said. Sid cast a glare at the colossal creature which showed off a sharp-toothed grin without remorse.

"Since you're here," Sid began as he hoisted the body into the seat of the chair and spun it so that the back was to the door in case someone was to walk in, "I have some questions for you."

"And what makes you think I'll answer them?"

Sid remembered the plastic beaded necklace that was still around his neck. "I have your amulet. And I'm not giving it back until you answer my questions."

The voice inside Sid's head sighed, annoyed, before taking a casual seat in another available chair, one on the other side of the desk from where the body was seated. "I can't kill you since you're the one that summoned me, so if that's the only way to get my amulet back, ask me anything you want, I guess."

With this little bit of information, Sid suddenly felt far more powerful. "So you can't kill me, huh? Any other special privileges?"

"Wait, you didn't know the terms of the summoning before you performed the ritual?"

"Um...no."

"It's all right there in the book."

"I didn't read it."

"Well then how—"

"*I'm* the one asking the questions here," Sid interrupted.

Killgrath sighed again, rubbing an exasperated clawed hand across his forehead between his ram horns. "I can't believe I'm bound to an idiot."

"Hey, you're the one who got us into this mess—wait, bound, you say? So you have to do what I tell you?"

"More or less...*with* the understanding that I *will* get the amulet back."

"Right, right, the amulet." Sid waved a hand in the air dismissively. Then he remembered the case he was on that led him to summon a demon in the first place. "So what's with all those people that died? Eyes melted out of their sockets? That couldn't have been you, could it?"

Killgrath laughed evilly. "The summoning only works every hundred times. I have a cult, you know. They offer themselves as sacrifices by the hundreds until I may offer my services to them."

"And I just happened to be the hundredth."

Killgrath nodded, and Sid was suddenly extremely grateful that he was in his current predicament and still had his eyes...and his life, for that matter. "You seem very proud of this," Sid mentioned.

"I am. Why wouldn't I be?"

"I guess you would be," Sid mused, "Prince of the Underworld and all that."

"Archduke," Killgrath corrected.

"Whatever." Sid thought for a moment. "Well, that's my case solved, I guess. Now we just need to figure out what the hell to do with *that*." He gestured toward the chair where the body was still slumped.

"Frame it as a suicide?" Killgrath offered nonchalantly.

Sid looked off into the distance, thinking. "Yes...yes, I could do that. But how?"

He glanced at his gun holsters hanging on the coat rack in the corner and got an idea. An awful, terrible idea. But one that would work.

Probably.

He got out the phone book he kept in his desk drawer and opened it up. Ada... What was her last name? Black...something? He scanned every name in the B's for anyone named Ada. And...*aha!* Ada J. Blackburn, 44

Sycamore. Perfect. Except for the fact that there was a "Mrs." next to her name. So she was married.

Damn it.

"Murder-suicide?" Killgrath offered from over Sid's shoulder.

Sid must have muttered under his breath without realizing. "It'll have to be, I guess. I don't feel good about killing another innocent human being, though."

"No human is really innocent," Killgrath said.

Sid rolled his eyes. "Okay, Edgar Allan Poe. Possess the body again, please, so we can get this over with." He showed the creature a map of the area and pointed out where he should take the body, since Sid would have to leave a few minutes later so as to mitigate suspicion.

Killgrath did as he was asked, walking the body downstairs. Thankfully, 44 Sycamore was only a few blocks away, which made for fewer people to see the clumsy walk of the possessed body, made worse due to the fact that rigor mortis was setting in. It was the wrong hour for such a totter to be explained away by inebriation, and therefore, it had to be over quickly.

Killgrath eventually got to the front door of 44 Sycamore and tried the doorknob.

Of course, it was locked.

Key. Key. Where do humans keep keys? Killgrath thought with all his might and couldn't come up with a solution better than standing there and waiting for Sid and his human brain to come help him.

"Hey there, Ada!" A cheerful voice grated on Killgrath's borrowed ears, and as he looked toward the adjacent yard to the left, he saw another human female approaching the door of the house adjacent to it, bearing a ring of keys in one hand and a purse slung across the other shoulder. "Forgot your purse?" *Purse. Of course that's where a human would keep their keys.*

Killgrath shrugged the body's shoulders and nodded with a forced smile. At this point, he could barely move the mouth at all due to the seized muscles.

"It's alright," the other woman giggled as she approached, rounding the hedge that divided the two properties. "I'll just use the spare you gave me, and then you can repay me with mimosas sometime."

Killgrath had no idea what a mimosa was, but he kept the forced smile on the body's face, simply grateful that this woman was here at exactly the right moment.

The woman unlocked the door and opened it for him, and he responded with a nod of gratitude. But as she got close to the body, her nose crinkled in disgust. "Have you been dumpster diving or something? You smell awful. Like...like rancid meat."

Uh oh. The body had now been dead for almost twelve hours without preservation of any kind and had just been walking in the sun for a solid half hour. It was rotting; time was running out.

Killgrath quickly stepped inside the house and closed the door without a word, dropped the body into a nearby living chair, and exorcised himself, pacing the floor in waiting for the detective to arrive.

The detective did arrive in due time with a knock at the door. Killgrath didn't understand why he would knock rather than just entering, but he quickly remembered the nosy neighbor he just dealt with and decided that Sid knew what was best in these situations. He was his reference for human behavior.

So Killgrath possessed the body again, just to walk it to the door and answer it.

Sid flashed his police badge. "Just a show for the neighbors. We wouldn't want any more suspicion placed on us." He pushed his way inside past the body, which shambled back over to the chair in which it was previously sitting and collapsed into it yet again, rigid against the seat. "Is the husband here yet?"

"No," replied Killgrath.

"Damn. I wanted to get this over with quickly. I don't want to spend more time here than I have to. Especially not hanging around a dead body." He then had to think for a moment before coming upon a sudden realization. "He's probably at work. And it's...ten after eight. We're going to have to wait a while. The neighbors are going to be suspicious if they're as nosy as I think they are."

"They are quite nosy," Killgrath confirmed.

"Great. So. What's a good reason for me to be here for so long?" Sid threw the question out into the open hoping that something would stick to it.

"Perhaps... An affair?" Killgrath said with an entertained grin.

Sid thought for a moment. "Ada would never in a million years go for a scumbag like me. But...it is the only thing that makes sense. I suppose we could go with that." He snapped his fingers with an idea. "And that would be the motive for the murder-suicide! Killgrath, you're a genius."

And so, they waited. For several hours. Sid made a tuna fish sandwich out of ingredients he found in the kitchen, and found the smell was just barely enough to wash out the stench of decaying flesh if he ate it far enough away from the living room. He also made himself coffee using the coffee machine, which fascinated Killgrath to no end. The demonic growling sounds of the boiling water delighted him and reminded him of home.

Finally, 5 o'clock rolled around, and so did a car into the driveway. Sid got into position on the couch in the living room and waited. Killgrath stood looming in the corner of the room just to observe, knowing full well that he wouldn't be seen no matter what, so it didn't particularly matter where he was.

The sound of footsteps on the porch approaching the door made Sid almost break into a sweat. He had never killed someone before, not even in the line of duty. He wasn't sure if he could handle it.

But he had to. For his own good.

The door opened, and in walked the Husband. Prim and proper in appearance, wearing his work suit. A guy straight out of a magazine ad. "Honey? Are you home?" he called. "You didn't answer my calls today..." He trailed off as he finally looked up and saw the scene before him: his wife, sitting slouched and very, very limp with eyes wide open in a chair next to a stranger on the couch, staring right at him, as though he were expecting him.

The Husband's eyes fixed on his wife's body. "Ada?"

"So...I feel like I should explain some things to you," Sid began in the calmest voice he could possibly muster as he pulled out his badge and showed it to him.

"What's wrong with her?" the Husband asked, "Is she alright?"

"Well, here's the thing. She's kind of... dead."

"*What*?!" the Husband dropped his briefcase and began to rush toward the body before Sid stood and stopped him. "When—who —how—" The Husband stuttered several beginnings-of-sentences before Sid interrupted him.

"Hey. Listen. This is all going to sound really weird, but I'm going to tell you exactly what happened, and what's *going* to happen, if you just...sit down over there, okay?"

There was a silence as the Husband glanced at Sid, complete and utter horror in his eyes, and then back at the body, before he nodded and sat down on the other end of the couch from where Sid had stood, and to where he was now returning.

"Okay. So. I've had a really weird day—" Sid said.

"*You've* had a really weird day?!" the Husband couldn't stop himself from shouting.

"Okay, okay. Yes, I know. This is hard for you. But let me explain."

The Husband exhaled the breath he was holding in disdain, nodded, and gestured for Sid to continue.

"So, I guess, long story short, I sort of accidentally summoned a demon that killed your wife."

The Husband's face was blank for a moment before he stood once again. "Okay. That's it. I'm going to get in contact with the Chief of Police and have you fired. *If* that badge even is real—" he had gotten to the door and his hand was on the doorknob when a familiar *crack* was heard. The Husband froze in place, his eyes rolled back in his head, and he fell to the floor.

"Disconnected the—?"

"Brain stem from the spinal cord," Killgrath confirmed.

"Great. Well, that went about as smoothly as it could. Now. This part is going to be tricky. We have to stage the scene."

"Meaning?"

"We have to make it look like a murder-suicide. We can't just leave them here. Help me bring them to the bedroom."

Killgrath did as was asked, although moving Ada was a difficult task due to her fully stiffened tissues. Ada's body was laid on the mattress, while Killgrath stood the body of the Husband up by the foot of the bed.

"Alright. Now is the time, I guess," Sid said, taking his gun out of his holster, standing next to the Husband's body, and aiming at Ada's.

He shot, and the amount of blood that still came out of the body was nauseating. And he would have to do that again.

He took the Husband's hand and positioned it to fire the gun, the barrel directly touching the underside of the husband's chin. Again, the gun fired, blood and brain matter splattering against the chest of drawers and wall behind him.

Sid dropped the gun, and Killgrath exited the body. "That hurt," he remarked.

"Too bad," Sid said with a curt glare. "Time to get out of here."

Sid put on his best terrified face as he ran out the front door and got into his car, quickly getting on his radio and making an emergency call to the station. It was only after he had done that when he realized how much blood had gotten on him. His first instinct was to go home and shower and change, but he figured it would be better for the narrative that he was trying to set if he had been there.

He also realized after that that, despite the fact that all this was mostly a façade, his hands were shaking violently. He had never shot anyone before. He had to remind himself that the Husband was already dead, and he still had never technically killed anyone, but with Killgrath possessing the body, it all felt so real. Like he was the perpetrator of this crime. Then again, he was probably liable for both of their deaths anyway, seeing as there was no precedent for prosecuting a literal demon.

Sid heard the sirens before he saw the flashing lights of the patrol cars that zoomed into the scene. As they stopped in front of the house, he got out of his car with his hands up and his badge showing.

Everything was a blur after that. Sid was taken in for questioning, Killgrath hovering around him the entire time, sometimes with an evil smile full of schadenfreude that was incredibly distracting.

At one point, as he was sitting alone in the interrogation room, Sid realized something. "Why are you still here?" he asked, making a point not to look anywhere in particular or to speak very loudly, knowing that he was still being monitored. "Don't you have anywhere you need to be?"

"You summoned me," Killgrath reminded him, "I am bound to you until you cast the spell to send me back to the underworld... which will also kill you."

Sid blinked. "Excuse me?"

Killgrath sighed. "Another thing you didn't know before carelessly summoning a demon. Yes, the freeing spell requires the sacrifice of the original summoner."

"That...would have been useful information," Sid mumbled.

"It was in the book."

Sid cast a cursory glare at Killgrath.

"Which you didn't read," Killgrath finished for him. "Well, I hope you've learned your lesson."

Sid kept his story the same for hours and hours of questioning: he and Ada were having an affair and were caught one night when time had slipped away from them, and Ada's husband came home from work. He caught them in the act, which is when Sid tried to deescalate the situation, but the husband wasn't having it, stole Sid's gun, and shot Ada before turning the gun on himself out of guilt.

"Why didn't he shoot you too?" Sid was asked several times. He didn't have an answer; it was a question he hadn't thought of being asked before orchestrating this whole thing.

More hours later, Sid was let go due to a lack of evidence proving he had anything to do with the case other than being an unfortunate witness. The only real witness, aside from the nosy neighbors who heard two gunshots, one right after the other, and then saw Sid running out of the house into his car.

Sid went home, Killgrath sitting in the passenger seat. He went straight to bed, Killgrath up and wandering around his apartment while he was sleeping.

Sid hadn't slept in a good thirty-six hours, but he still had trouble falling asleep. He couldn't get over the feeling of lukewarm blood splattering over him, how it all just...sprayed everywhere. He had always imagined blood to be thicker than that somehow.

And when he finally was able to close his eyes, every time he was on the verge of actual sleep, he felt the sudden shock of the gun firing in his hand and the incredibly loud sound it made ringing in his ears. Furthermore, it didn't help that every so often when he would open his eyes, glowing red pupils would stare at him from the darkness of his room. He knew it was Killgrath, he knew he would come to no harm, and yet there was something incredibly unsettling about it. Maybe it set off a metaphor in his mind of the fact that he would eventually be caught. The perps always got caught; that was just the way it was. He might be able to plead insanity due to the fact that a demon was his accomplice, but ultimately, he pulled the trigger both times and he would have to live with that in a mental institution even if he didn't get the death penalty.

It was then that he realized, perhaps sacrificing himself to send Killgrath back to the underworld wouldn't be the worst option.

After a night of restless sleep, he got out of bed at 5 a.m., prepared to sneak into his office and take the book home with him. Thankfully, nobody was at the station yet (he and Ada were the only ones likely to stay late anyway) so he was in and out without a problem.

At home, he decided to take the time to actually read the book. A lot of it was nonsense about an eternity in paradise, ruling over the dead, ultimate power, *et cetera, et cetera*. Although, really, at this point, how could he rule any of it out, knowing that demons were real? At least this one was. Or maybe he had finally snapped and gone insane. Maybe he really *had* killed Ada and her husband, and Killgrath was an invention of his psychotic mind that protected him from the truth and reality of the situation.

"I am real," Killgrath's voice echoed in Sid's mind. "I can assure you that." Of course he could read Sid's mind.

"That's exactly what a figment of my imagination would say," Sid retorted.

"That is true, isn't it?" Killgrath thought out loud, or at least as "out loud" as he could be.

"So, if all I have to do is kill myself, why don't I just do it? Is it really that easy?"

"The circle."

"What?"

"You have to draw the circle first."

Sid flipped to the relevant page in the book, looked at the design of the circle, and groaned. That was the most complicated thing he had ever seen with his own two eyes. At least it would give him time to think back on his life while he was drawing.

He hadn't had very many accomplishments. Graduating from the police academy was one thing, but he had barely scraped by on all his tests. Just like he had barely scraped by on *all* his tests, even before the academy. All throughout school, he did the bare minimum. All throughout his life, he did the bare minimum. Just enough to keep his job and his apartment. He never once thought he would end up doing what he was doing now.

He finished the drawing, gave one final look around his apartment, and said a silent goodbye before turning his gun on himself for a final shot.

Or, at least, he thought that's how it would go.

After a loud bang and a sharp pain shooting through his head, he soon realized that he was still conscious. He opened his eyes and saw that there was no blood anywhere. Not on the walls, on the furniture, or on himself.

He looked around for Killgrath, and saw the demon standing in the corner, looking just as baffled as Sid was.

"What happened? Am I still alive?" Sid asked.

"I...I don't know," Killgrath answered, "Maybe... you did the wrong ritual?"

Sid looked down at the circle he drew, looking for any kind of inconsistency in the way he drew it versus the way it looked in the book, and he did finally locate a discrepancy...

He flipped through the pages again, scouring them for any sign of another circle that was similar but different in effect, and found one.

A ritual for immortality.

"No," Sid muttered, "No, no, no, I can't live forever, that's not the way this is supposed to go." He had to think quickly. He knew his neighbors heard the gunshot and would be on their way to check on him at any second. "We have to get out of town, now."

Sid didn't even bother packing a bag; he just left the apartment, ignoring his next-door neighbor who emerged to ask him if he was alright.

He got in his car and drove. He picked a direction—east—and stepped on the gas.

Then he remembered the demon in his passenger seat. "So this really means we're stuck together forever now, huh?"

Killgrath thought about the amulet, and how Sid had apparently forgotten that he was still wearing it. He thought about the fact that if he could just obtain the amulet, he could go back to the underworld, to the way things used to be.

But the way things used to be were boring.

"I suppose we are," the demon said.

Timeless

by R.L. Pace

In the gloom of the primordial forest OotMa the Timeless One walked with a steady stride and sure gait stepping over twigs and around stones without hesitation. Her walking stick of healing willow was well worn and her hand held fast to the seal skin leather loop. For millenia and more, beyond memory, she had journeyed with her people across the frozen reaches from one continent to another, seen her tribes grow and prosper even as glaciers melted away in the new lands.

She had rowed with warriors in cedar canoes across the straits between islands and mainland and watched a ship commanded by George Vancouver as it sailed near her family village of Bahaada. In the ancientness of her life the Timeless One had fished for salmon and halibut, harpooned whales and fashioned clothing from cedar bark and sea otter skins.

She had been present, but untouched, as disease ravaged her people and been an honored elder when her tribes finally bowed to the treaty seventy five years ago. She had lived the length of a thousand lives and more, yet she had seen nothing with her own eyes. OotMa was born blind and the world was invisible to her without a keeper of the vision quest. Death touched everyone in its time—her time —including countless vision keepers, but it had not yet beckoned for the Timeless One.

ᘉ

October 1927

Makah Indian Village

Neah Bay, Wash.

"Watch where we are going, child! Pay attention to the path ahead, you are looking for both of us." OotMa said.

"I am trying, OotMa. It's hard! I like to see through the birds." Bird Far Seeing was barely fourteen and like all young boys dreaming of becoming great hunters he chafed at being stuck with looking out for the village's oldest citizen. Literally looking, in his case. He had only begun his studies as a Keeper and the only vision quest on his mind at the moment was being with his friends preparing to become a warrior.

"Stop then. Come here, boy. Let me see what you see. First, close your eyes." OotMa opened her mind and gently laid her consciousness upon her young acolyte like a cloud enveloping a high mountain peak. After generations of training new vision quest students she knew this could be an unsettling experience for them, suddenly having another voice not your own in your head. "Open your eyes and let me see."

Bird Far Seeing opened his eyes and looked at OotMa.

That's right. Now I see myself as you see me.

Suddenly there was a jarring, almost kaleidoscopic image of her left ear in a hundred tiny identical pictures, then just as suddenly it was replaced with another view of the two of them from somewhere higher, a tree branch perhaps. *What are you doing? What vision is this?* OotMa had never in her centuries beheld such a sight.

"I saw a fly on your shoulder, and then a jay in the tree." He said aloud.

Speak to me with your mind. You saw me through their eyes?

Yes, OotMa, he thought. *I have always seen through other eyes. It's how I got my name. If I can see any creature, I can look through their eyes.*

Show me the eyes of the eagle up there in the sky, she commanded.

He turned and focused his attention on the bird soaring high above wondering how she knew there was one up there.

There is always an eagle in the sky on a clear day, she explained.

Now their shared field of vision became an aerial view of the lush temperate rain forests on the earth below and the unseasonably clear sky above them. At first it was dizzying and exhilarating to OotMa as she fought to make sense of what her young student was showing her. Then it was instantly terrifying. Through the eyes of the eagle they could see a column of thick black smoke rising from the direction of their village. Poised overhead hovering just above the tops of the cedars and Sitka spruce was a massive black dirigible airship.

The Timeless One extended her thoughts to the predatory brain of the eagle and though she couldn't be certain, his telescopic vision seemed to reveal a rain of death issuing from underneath the dark leviathan.

Run, little bird. We must run to the village as fast as we can. Look only through your eyes at the path ahead and run! Together they ran through the forest amid the towering giants, nearly silent on the evergreen straw beneath their feet, across the creeks for their home at the edge of the world.

From a hidden position behind a fallen log at the edge of the village OotMa spoke to Bird Far Seeing in his mind. *We must see the great canoe of the sky. Keep hidden, but find a way.* Bird squinted through the branches, then spotted a raven perched on a limb near the Elders Lodge. The Timeless One extended her mind and through the eyes of the raven searched each direction until the massive airship came into view. It was enormous, all black save some elements of the gondola. Upon its aft vertical stabilizer a large four point silver star was visible and near the forward nose was printed *Nephthys*.

Nephthys slowly settled close to the clearing where fishing nets were mended and four people wearing black uniforms slid down ropes dangling from the basket. Once on the ground they tied the airship off to nearby trees and the sound of grinding winches could be heard as the ship pulled itself to the earth.

Responding to the nudges of OotMa, the raven took flight, circling near, as a short gangplank was lowered and heavily armed troops rolled out. Through raven the hidden pair could see a woman with glistening golden hair and very fair skin speaking and pointing toward areas not already afire. The troops dispersed to the spots indicated and moments later the blasts of gunfire and terrified wailing was heard, only to fall silent at the report of another gunshot.

The raven perched on the outstretched wings of the great lodge totem eagle and viewed the scene curiously. Presently two of the troopers dragged a man to the ship and dropped him at the feet of the blond woman. She lifted his chin with the toe of her boot and spoke. His response drew a savage kick to his face and the two troopers lifted him and tied him to the opposite totem. Again the woman spoke, again the response drew a rain of blows. This was repeated until the man could no longer respond, hanging limply from his bindings.

More commands were issued and back-packed equipment was brought from the belly of the ship. Teams dispersed throughout the village. Fire belched in molten incendiary orange streams until everything was ablaze right to the edge of the cold waters of the Pacific Ocean. When OotMa released raven, Bird Far Seeing peeked over the windfall where they were shielded from view. The last of the troops re-boarded the *Nephthys*, cast off the lines, and the ship drifted skyward as the thrum of her thruster engines filled the air.

The pair of hidden witnesses made their way into the village to the totem where the man sagged inert. Bird cut his bindings and laid him on the ground where OotMa ministered to his grievous wounds.

"What did they want?" She asked. "Why did they come here and destroy our village and our people? What were they looking for?"

"Immortality, OotMa. The secret to everlasting life. They were looking for you, Timeless One."

∞

One Week Later in New York City

The last man David Li expected-or wanted-to see standing in his Tribeca brownstone at seven a.m. was Joe Frankels. It was Frankels, the Shanghai bureau chief for AEGIS that had given him the assignment that put a Chinese tong on his tail which very nearly snuffed him out in San Francisco. And after the most re-cent bloody affair just blocks from his home that had killed an associate and netted him a new partner, Li was hoping for some ordinary gumshoe work that made a few quick bucks without risking going up in smoke or ending up in the East River wearing cement over-shoes.

"Joe Frankels, as I barely live and breathe. What brings you to Gotham all the way from Shanghai?"

Frankels huffed. "I'll give you the short ver-sion: Transferred to HQ, new chief of security. Pack a bag, we have a plane standing by and a training assignment that we think your spe-cial, uh, gifts, can benefit from."

Not many knew of the psychic manipula-tions and ectoplasmic extension Li was capa-ble of, and that was as he liked it. That the Al-lied Enterprise Group for International Securi-ty wanted to put him in a position where those capabilities were on full display was exactly the opposite of what he had in mind.

"Just like that? Pack a bag? Where, might I ask, am I going?" Li did not like the direction this conversation was taking.

"Seattle," Joe replied. "I'm sorry David, I know you had asked to be put on the shelf for a while, but we need more help. Besides, there might be some first rate detective work for you as well. And you did say you wanted some help developing those talents of yours."

Sigh...Frankels is no fool and he knows I can't resist a front loaded compliment. Li briefly used his powers to reach out mentally, feeling the texture of the switch with his mind and started the coffee pot sitting near the sink with a loud click. *May as well get a jolt of java before I go.* "Let me call Betsy. She'll need to take over the case load while I'm away."

"Miss Schneider has been made aware. We have assigned someone to help her out and cover her six. You won't have time for coffee," Joe said, reaching over and turning off the pot. "We really do need to be on the way."

"Bum's rush is it? Okay then. Let me throw something together. How long am I going to be gone?"

"Not sure, David, but plan for a couple of weeks at least. You won't need neckties or dress shoes, but warm socks and a good fedora to shed the rain would be a plus. And don't forget your marbles."

Li tossed together some items in a battered leather suitcase and placed a selection of steel ball bearings in three different pockets. His most recent experience suggested plain marbles just weren't imbued with enough punch.

In less than an hour he was airborne on the first leg of what would prove to be another exhausting relay cross-country to Seattle.

CR

Li had never been to the northwest corner of the U.S. except in transit and he turned up the collar of his trench coat against the biting wind and cold evening drizzle that greeted him. Several hundred miles north of New York's latitude, Seattle was already nearly dark. The rendezvous point was the Freeman Hotel in what passed for a Chinatown in Seattle.

David stepped off the platform at King Street Station, and though he had managed to grab a nap during the journey he felt the need to stretch his legs. He used his special powers to mentally feel for the reassuring presence of the steelies in his jacket pocket. Something he could shoot like a bullet with his mind should the need arise. The East Yick building which housed the hotel was only a few blocks away in the International District so he consulted his street map and headed out. In the gloaming he barely noticed two men fall in behind him. Taking long, easy strides moving between the pools of dim amber streetlight in ten minutes flat, he hit the hotel and climbed to the second floor lobby.

His first thought was how much he looked forward to a decent night's sleep. Then he saw the tall blond woman in the *Astrum Argentum* uniform and felt a needle plunge into his neck. His last thought was *I am really sick of being knocked out from behind.*

℞

"Wake up, mister!" Li tried to focus on the sound of the voice. *Must be dreaming,* he thought. *Sounds like a kid.*

"C'mon, mister, you gotta wake up!" David could feel his body being shaken. *Gawd Li, do an assessment. What seems to be working?* Tentatively he opened his eyes, only to blink back the glare of bright illumination emanating from what he judged to be the ceiling.

"Mr. Li, you must awaken yourself."

He looked up to see a young boy and a woman leaning over him.

"Please, we will need to work together to escape." The two helped him into a seated position on the floor while he tried to wave away the cobwebs clouding his brain.

He knew this feeling. It was the same drug Sheng had used on him at the Mind Mists club back home in New York. That fact alone was sobering and he went through a mental checklist.

"Help me up," he asked the kid. On his feet the room seemed to career as he steadied himself. "My name...wait, how do you know my name?"

"I am OotMa of the Makah. I am also called the Timeless One. I am the reason you are here. Well, not here exactly, but in Seattle. This is Bird Far Seeing. He is my vision quest."

Vision quest? Timeless One? None of this made any sense to Li. She offered a brief explanation of her blindness and Bird's role as her vision quest.

"Our village was destroyed, we escaped to Seattle and found AEGIS to ask for an investigation, but somehow Silver Star found us and now we are prisoners."

"Fat lot of good I'm gonna be. I can't even seem to protect myself." David looked around. They were in a small room that was absolutely featureless save for a built in bench and table seemingly molded into the space. The light glowed from the ceiling but not from any fixture. The walls and floor were a seamless light gray. No visible door, no hint of a window. Not a single loose item with any mass or size at all. No overcoat, no bearings.

This is seriously not good. This room seems designed specifically to make my mental powers nearly useless. The Silver Star knew I was coming. "Why was I coming to see you? Why me and not someone else less likely to get clunked on the head?" *If I get out of this alive Frankels is going to have a lot of explaining to do.*

"I was told you have a special gift you wished to understand better. Perhaps you could show me this gift."

"If you have a small object I can demonstrate the effect. It's the only way I know of to 'show' it."

Bird Far Seeing produced a piece of sheepskin from his pocket attached to which was a large fish hook. The guards had apparently neglected to search the kid. "Will this do?"

David reached out with his powers and gently separated the hook by moving aside with his mind all the hairs holding it in place then lifted it a foot above everyone and sent it in a circle around their heads, setting it back down on the pad. Then he oozed a tiny filament of ectoplasm from his finger which he directed through the eye of the hook, looping it into a knot. He used the result to cast the hook across the room, then drew his element back into himself depositing the hook once again onto the wool.

"I see," OotMa said. "Very unusual. What do your powers tell you about this room?"

Li released his mind and began probing every joint and all of the walls. He could feel mechanisms that were likely some kind of door, but they were hopelessly complex. It would take hours to decipher and far more energy than he had, given the effects of the drugs that still lingered. There were seams at the walls and ceiling but rather than being components they seemed to be a single uniform material. Welded perhaps. He could discern nothing about the light source of the ceiling at all. The one other thing he noticed was that there seemed to be movement of some kind. And a faint humming sound when he fully opened his mind.

"My powers tell me we will have to wait for someone to open the door. Now, hows about you telling me a little something about your powers? And just how old can you be to be called the Timeless One? You look to be mid-thirties at the oldest. She made a brief explanation of her blindness and Bird Far Seeing's role as her eyes.

"And you look like you need to sit down. Let me tell you my story..."

 C๛

Out of uniform Arngerd Janssen looked like the spawn of an ice goddess. Her golden locks cascaded beyond her shoulders. Her cerulean eyes glittered like sapphires set in pale, translucent skin above high cheekbones. Wearing a navy blue pullover sweater and sleek matching gabardine trousers she was a study in Nordic beauty and she used it to her advantage whenever it suited her. And it suited her now.

"Tell me, Captain," she purred. "How are our guests enjoying the vault?

"It's hard to tell. They can't see out, we can't see in. The specifications were quite precise in that regard." Percy Smythe was always slightly awkward around women, more so if they happened to be uncommonly attractive. Before swearing fealty to Alistair Crowley and Silver Star he had been a Royal Navy lifer, now he was captain of an airship of the line, the *Nephthys*, and taking orders from this woman half his age. He fingered his collar and continued. "We know Detective Li hasn't attempted to escape or unlock the vault mechanism. Presumably they are waiting."

"It's been six hours, by now the effects of the drugs have worn off. How long until we reach the landing site?"

"Within minutes. That's what I came to tell you. Despite the delay caused by the earlier headwinds and rain we'll be moored and ready to begin well before dusk."

"Excellent! Have them prepare the altar as soon as we are tied off. I will have Kurt bring the instruments."

"Very well, Miss Janssen."

"Smile, Captain. We are about to achieve literal immortality." Smythe saluted perfunctorily and turned to leave thinking *Immortality might be a curse, not a blessing.*

CR

David Li had noticed the cessation of the slight hum and could no longer detect any motion. While some uncertainty existed he estimated that it probably meant the status quo was about to change.

"I think we've stopped." He said. "Whatever they have planned for us is gonna happen soon." No sooner had he spoken than an opening whispered into view. Beyond that stood half a dozen Silver Star agents wielding machine guns, clad in black uniforms but distorted by a shimmering glow surrounding each of them. Leading them was the Ice Goddess herself, wrapped in her own glowing aura.

"Mr. Li, as you can see, we are well prepared for you and your powers. It's a pity, really. You could be so useful to us."

Li's mind raced. The auras seemed to be some mechanical version of the powers he had encountered in his previous tangle with the Golden Dragon Tong at the Mind Mists Club in New York. It wasn't a pleasant memory. An associate had died and he had very nearly come to pushing up daisies himself. That Silver Star had obviously spent so much effort to thwart him in particular suggested they knew more about the role AEGIS had in mind for him than he did.

With the Ice Goddess leading the way Bird, OotMa and Li fell into step between the phalanx formed by the rest of the guards. Almost immediately it seemed to David as though their progress was just slightly off kilter. The guards were taking full strides, but they seemed slowed somehow, like trying to walk through water but not as pronounced. Every few steps he would have to half-step to keep the space the same. *This seems odd,* he thought, *maybe it's the effect of the force field.*

Through the eyes of Bird Far Seeing the Timeless One was making her own assessment. Down the passageway they marched past armed guards blocking access hatches, each one focusing on the golden haired woman as they passed. OotMa sensed fear and occasionally lust but saw nothing likely to aid them.

As they reached the forward exit from the gondola where the gangway was open the group halted as the Captain stepped out to speak.

"Your orders, Ma'am?"

"When we are debarked take her up to five hundred feet and stand off another thousand. We'll send up a flare when we are ready for re-covery."

"As you wish." The captain retreated to the bridge

Well, at least that will change our odds from hopeless to just overwhelming, Li thought.

CR

Equipment, and what appeared to be an altar of some kind, had already been off-loaded. Men in lab coats were striding purposefully about pointing and giving instructions to Silver Star technicians. A large generator had hawser-thick wires connected to five glistening metallic pyramidal objects, each about eight feet tall. Between them markings had been made creating a pentagram shape and inside the center of that stood the ceremonial table. Five tall slender metal poles, each placed corresponding to a point on the pentagram, held aloft a chromium sphere about a yard in diameter above the altar. The sphere and the pyramids were etched in figures and symbols. It all looked impressive to David. And dangerous.

"Well, Timeless One. We finally meet." Janssen had a look of triumph in her eyes.

"You needn't have destroyed the village," OotMa replied. "That was cruel." *Let me see through each person's eyes, Bird. But say nothing aloud.*

"Perhaps, but I like the theater of it. Must set an example to establish my authority."

"To whom? My people offered no threat."

"Oh the demonstration wasn't for your village. It was for mine." She gestured to the workers and armed guards, then remembering her captive was blind dropped her arm to her side in irritation. "It never hurts to remind staff that failure will not be tolerated."

"And who will not tolerate your failure? Alistair Crowley?"

The Ice Queen leaned in close to OotMa's face and growled *sotto voce* "When I am finished here Crowley will answer to me."

"What do you believe you will gain with your cruelty?"

"Why I am surprised," Janssen replied, "haven't you heard? You're the guest of honor. I mean to take your longevity from you and give it to myself. I'm looking forward to living forever."

"I think you will not find the face of eternity to your liking."

Bird Far Seeing had been systematically giving his mentor a look through the eyes of every technician and guard, and with her prodding had lingered over the control station near the generator and the inscriptions on the objects forming the enclosed area.

Meanwhile, David Li, content to be ignored for the moment, had been doing his own mental reconnaissance, probing for weaknesses in the shielded guards and the surroundings as far as his powers could reach. So far he had found none, which was worrisome to say the least.

As they were prodded forward a light mist began to envelop the group and the last feeble light of the day disappeared, leaving the assembly in the harsh glare of electric arc lights run by a noisy generator set up some distance from the perimeter.

One of the lab coated men detached himself from his group and approached Janssen. "Everything is in order and ready to begin the trial run," he announced.

"Splendid, Kurt. Proceed as planned."

"*Jawol sofort, mein Priesterin der Dunkelheit.*" The man hurried back to his station and made a signal which apparently meant 'let's go' as everyone began assuming positions around the varied equipment.

"You see," Janssen intoned, "my demonstration in your useless village has had the desired effect. They immediately obey their Priestess of Darkness."

"Fear is a poor substitute for loyalty. It has no endurance in the long race and no power when its weakness is exposed." OotMa's exploration of the markings on the equipment through Bird Far Seeing seemed familiar, but from a time so long ago its clarity was shrouded even from her.

The Ice Goddess sneered her irritation but said nothing. Presently an oblong box was opened and two technicians struggled awkwardly to extract a limp body from its confines and carry it over to the altar. David Li was startled to see it was a young woman, completely naked. Once upon the pedestal they draped her with a cloth covered with more hieroglyphics and attached electrodes to her feet, hands, and head. He tried extending his powers to test the bonds but they were too far away for his efforts. *At least she's unconscious for this. Or dead.*

From behind a low control station shielded with thick glass Kurt turned a dial to its midpoint. In the distance the generator responded with a mechanical groan and higher engine revs to meet the increased demand for current. The outer perimeter pyramids began to glow, their markings changing from a metallic tone to an ominous carmine red hue. He turned the control knob to seventy-five percent. There was no apparent effect.

Then suddenly a brilliant flash of light turned night into daylight as a streak of energy coursed from the globe into the inert figure on the table. Nearly instantly the altar was empty. No naked woman, no cloak, no scorch marks of any kind. OotMa focused her mind on the dials Kurt was looking at. The control dial was reset to zero, but another was steady at thirty percent. It was marked 'KONDEN-SATOR'. Kurt searched out Janssen's eyes and gave her a big smile and a thumbs up indication. A broad smile of triumph broke across her face.

"It works," she crowed. "I've no need for Crowley's demons. I'll have immortality! Prepare the boy!"

Two guards crossed over and seized Bird Far Seeing dragging him toward the altar, removing his clothes from his body as they went.

Do not resist these men. I will protect you. Do not be afraid.

No, OotMa, I am not afraid.

The Timeless One gently entered David Li's mind. Trying not to startle him, she whispered into his consciousness: *The moment is nearing when you must release your mind and your powers to me, David.*

"Wait! What?"

The Ice Princess turned at the outburst to study Li. *Do not speak aloud,* OotMa warned, *only with your mind!* Li gathered himself and stared back at the blond letting his dark brown eyes take on what he hoped was a helpless and hopeless mien. "Take me instead. He's only a kid." *Mr. Li, this is not my plan!*

"Oh, how very noble of you, David, rest assured, your turn will come. just not yet." She returned her attention to the efforts to put Bird onto the altar.

Maybe not, he thought back, *but you need a diversion and I can be a pretty good one when I have to be.*

You must release your powers to me.

You're inside my head, how can you not already control them?

Once more the generator thrummed up to meet a new load, and Li turned to look just as the blinding flash lit up the scene. Inside his head his mind exploded in a vortex of energy and he could feel his powers rising to levels he had no inkling he possessed.

With the strength of his mind—but not at his command—knobs flew off machines, stones the size of basketballs rocketed into guards, knocking them off their feet despite their force fields. Filaments flew from his fingertips attaching to something and yanking it free only to deposit it beyond the light line among the forest ferns. It all seemed instantaneous. So fast no one could really react. Oot-Ma stood silently beside the Priestess of Darkness whose mouth was agape in astonishment.

"Kurt!" She screamed, "What has happened?" The pedestal was empty. Only the cloak they had placed on Bird Far Seeing was still there. Equipment was in disarray, technicians collecting themselves to assess the situation.

"I don't know? I don't understand. Everything was working perfectly."

"What about the condenser?" Kurt looked at the dial, it still read thirty percent.

"Still the same. Nothing from the child, but nothing lost."

"Find him you stupid imbeciles," she screamed at the guards who were just regaining their breath. "Find the child and bring him back immediately." They scrambled to their feet and after some confusion searching for flashlights they fanned out into the surrounding forest.

"You don't need the child," OotMa intoned. "You want me. You seek to take what I cannot give. So take it now."

Like a scene change from in a grand opera the pieces of the set were repositioned, power cords reattached and technicians were back at their workstations. Most of the guards had returned, their search for Bird having been fruitless.

"Of course, you are correct. The boy was merely another test, a bit more energy, so to speak. But I can claim that whenever I choose. So I grant your wish, old woman. I will take you now.

What are your doing? Are you nuts? This crazy woman will kill you! Li hoped the panic in his thoughts was evident.

All things die in their time, Mr. Li. But be hopeful, where there is life there is strength. Now please, look at the cloak and focus your attention. I must see it clearly. OotMa had never tried to look through the eyes of an untrained adult. But look she must this time.

The Timeless One was led toward the altar by the technicians. She shed her garments as she walked and took up the altar robe, wrapping herself carefully, absorbing its ancient runes and meanings, before lying down. Again the generator strained, the symbols glowed.

Arngerd leaned forward in anticipation; even the guards stared, waiting for the flash of light. But it did not come. Reaching once more into Li's mind OotMa directed a nearly invisible filament to turn the power dial to one hundred percent.

The arc lamps failed, plunging the area into near total darkness—only the glow of the symbols casting their eerie red glow lit the scene. Time seemed suspended and the robed figure of OotMa arose like Lazarus and reached over her head to grasp the chromium globe.

Transformed, she shone like a beacon, her eyes searchlights, her hands and feet pulsating. Releasing her grip, she floated to earth in front of the Priestess of Darkness who was rooted to the spot like the giant cedars of the forest.

"You seek eternal life. My life. Here it is." The Timeless one grasped her hands and stared into the icy blue eyes. "See what I have seen in my lifetime."

Janssen's body shuddered and became rigid as a thousand times a hundred years of death, disease, warfare and strife poured terror into her mind. "This is what you sought to take from me in a single moment. This is my gift to you in that moment."

A low keening wail began to emanate from the Ice Princess, becoming a raw, shrieking dirge possessed of lamentations beyond endurance, finally trailing away into a catatonic stare.

OotMa released her hands and withdrew from her mind. Janssen fell to the earth, inert. Turning her attention to the technicians and guards, OotMa surged up to the globe and struck it with her hands. Showers of sparks erupted like fireworks, cascading through the equipment carrying with it the fearsome reality of eternity. In the blink of an eye Silver Star personnel began collapsing in coruscating showers of their own, disappearing into the void leaving behind only their clothing.

As the Timeless One settled to earth, her body returned to the state David Li had known. The generator, no longer overburdened, powered the lights back to normal and Bird Far Seeing edged in from the forest. Each reclaimed their clothes with Bird and Li contemplating what they had just witnessed.

"So what happens now?" Li finally asked.

"We send up a flare. It's a long walk back to Seattle. By now AEGIS will have recovered *Nepthys*, discovered keeping station unmanned not far away."

"Excuse me for asking, but how did a blind —and forgive me, *old*—woman do all that?"

"I am disabled, Mr Li, Not disarmed. The oldest lesson of warfare is never to underestimate your opponent. Or overestimate yourself.

I could easily have failed had I not had access to your powers."

"Yeah, about that," Li began.

"That is a lesson for tomorrow, if you are willing. I think you will make a fine student."

"Okay, check. But remind me to never make you mad."

The Hunting Pack
by Todd Downing

The air was heavy and smelled of rotting meat, like the sultry breath of a gator in the bayou during high summer. Wet and weighed down as if the sky itself was a colossal duvet and the world beneath it a sick child swaddled in a sweltering cocoon by an overprotective matron. A blanket of primordial heat that made green things flourish, and pink and brown things simmer in their own fat.

Loana took note of the tiny rivulet of perspiration that ran from the nape of her neck down her right shoulder blade, making its way to the small of her back, but she did not move. Her olive complexion shone wet in the dappled sunlight of the jungle's edge. Her face a mask a feral instinct, eyes the color of garnet, chestnut locks cascading to her shoulders.

Her quarry, a spinosaur feasting on a fresh kill of its own, stopped in mid-bite and tested the air.

Loana was downwind, and absolutely silent. Eventually the creature relaxed and went back to its meal.

Like others of her tribe, Loana wore almost nothing, out of practicality. What little she did wear was functional in the extreme, and completely made from the remnants of her kills. A simple halter and loincloth of tanned iguanodon hide kept her vulnerable parts secure, a pair of wrapped boots armoring her lower legs against razor grass and smaller varieties of biting creatures. Her forearms were braced with twin prongs of sharpened bone, bound tightly with strips of dinosaur leather.

Her left shoulder bore the skull of some vanquished theropod, which acted as a kind of pauldron against attack from that side. Her right side was unencumbered in that regard, carrying only the bone shanks strapped to her arm, and a small arsenal of spears and javelins. Some were two-meter lengths of sharpened bone, like the skewers on her arms. Others were longer—three meters or more, hewn from native acacia trees, and capped with deadly spear points of chipped obsidian.

She crouched in the tall grass at the jungle mouth bordering the wetlands along a vast plain explorers from the outer world had named the Dinosaur Coast. A stream that began high in the mountains now meandered through some small, grassy dunes to the sea, providing fish with a handy spawning ground —and hungry spinosaurs with plenty of prey.

Every inch of Loana's suntanned frame was coiled vigilance. Spinosaurs were uncanny opponents, seemingly able to outguess the savviest of hunters. But they were also large and meaty, and could feed the entire extended tribe for a week or more. *If* she could avoid being snapped up by its giant crocodilian jaws, or slashed open by its front talons, or eviscerated by its dorsal sail, or crushed by its massive tail or muscular hind legs.

This particular spinosaur happened to be a huge specimen, seven meters tall at the shoulder and eighteen meters from nose to tail tip. A massive, lurching, eating machine that would seek no quarter, nor offer any.

Loana gripped the longest spear in a wrapped fist. She tensed, her leg muscles ready to spring.

Then she caught the tiniest motion in the scrub brush to her left, and knew she was no longer alone in this hunt.

The spinosaur reared back. It, too, had felt something change on the wind.

Instantly a large theropod of the raptor variety sprang from the mouth of the jungle, sprinting toward the spinosaur at top speed.

The massive quarry spun to face the oncoming threat, which angled its left hindquarters toward Loana.

Perfect, she thought, and leaped from the tall grass, spear in hand.

She cleared the sandy bank in a few swift strides, padding across the open marsh at top speed. Her breath was hot in her chest.

As she closed with the target, she made sure to keep her peripheral vision wide, tracking the raptor running in from the front. Suddenly, on her right, another of the same type of raptor came racing up the beach from behind a massive boulder. Loana knew that rock. It was a good hiding place. She'd only passed on it because she preferred the all-over camouflage of the tall grass near the jungle.

Then something fell into step slightly behind and to her left, and she knew without looking that a third raptor was keeping pace. It had probably tracked her for an hour or more, waiting in the shadows of the rainforest. Watching her. Waiting for her to lead its pack right to a prime kill.

After all, that was the plan.

Loana heard the strides of the beast on her left approach at twice her own speed. Timing on this maneuver had to be precise. She counted off the last three paces in her head and planted the butt of the long spear in the mossy ground, vaulting up and forward. The sprinting raptor was beneath her in a moment, and she landed softly on its back—right foot braced near the pelvis, left between its shoulder blades. The two moved as a nightmarish freight train, the charging theropod and its human rider, feral and bristling with weapons.

It had taken her a month to teach Spot this stunt. She'd had made it a priority, as it put her closer to a large target's vital zones.

The last hazard, of course, was the spinosaur's thrashing tail, which it whipped back and forth to protect its rear quarter. Using her evolved binocular vision, Loana saw the mighty appendage crack to the right like a whip and begin its snakelike return toward them. Tapping her left foot in her mount's shoulder blade, Loana crouched, almost a surfing stance. The spinosaur's tail cut a swathe of air in their direction. At the last possible moment, the raptor sprang into the heavy tropical air. Loana suddenly found herself at her quarry's shoulder level.

Leaping from her mount's shoulders, Loana sailed up, over the spinosaur's back, over the mass of coiled muscle and thick hide. She impacted its dorsal sail on its left side, sliding down to land atop its hunched shoulders with her full weight on the point of the long spear. It plunged deep into the back of the creature's neck. Another thrust with all of her might, and the spear popped through, out the front of its throat.

The spinosaur roared, and there was an audible gurgle in the sound.

Spot came down at the creature's left haunch, digging into sinews of flesh with his feathered talons and curved hind claws. The spinosaur twisted to face the source of its agony, to no avail. The other raptors vied for the giant theropod's attention, leaping and slicing at its forelimbs and right flank with hooked claws and furious, gnashing teeth.

Loana was glad they were on her side.

Pulling herself up from beneath the spear, she flung her legs over and around the back of the spinosaur's neck, now streaked with blood. Again the dinosaur reared and shrieked, almost shaking her off in the bargain.

Clenching both hands into fists, Loana pointed her arm-spikes inward, toward each other, two sharp points poised at each of the creature's reptilian eyes. She took a deep breath and plunged her arms toward the center of its head.

This was her killing blow, her finishing move. It rarely failed to bring down even the largest of prehistoric game. Once the bone-spikes penetrated the auditory canal and into the brain, there was usually not much fight left. But for some reason, the spinosaur wasn't getting the message that it was already dead.

Loana felt a spasm down the gargantuan spine, and the monster shook its head violently. Try as she might to keep her thighs clamped tightly at the beast's neck, the force was too great, and she found herself suddenly flung into the air toward the shallow inlet at its feet. She slapped the water and gasped with the impact, wind forced from her lungs. Stunned momentarily, she gazed up at the giant theropod, It was blind in one eye, bleeding from the head and throat, its cries gurgling and sputtering in the morning air.

Blood from Loana's own broken nose mixed with the brackish river water, painting her mouth and chin a marbled brown and red. She realized that the gauntlet which formerly housed the twin barbs on her right arm had been stripped from her, and now remained lodged in the beast's head, which it rattled from side to side in an almost deliriously defiant dance.

The massive predator crashed forward a single step, squinting through its one good eye, a thundering, sputtering roar emanating from its mighty crocodilian jaws. The pack of raptors assaulted it from all angles, but for the first time, Loana could see a determination in its glassy eye.

It stalked toward the lone human figure as she lay stunned in the river shallows a few short yards distant, shivering despite the heat. Leaning forward, its mouth snapped open, angry, glistening teeth on top and bottom, dripping bands of saliva between them. Another blood-curdling roar filled the wetlands, and Loana knew instinctively that her time was at an end. Her body tensed, bracing for impending doom.

The larger female raptor sprinted beneath the spinosaur's lowered neck and tore its throat out, which caused the dying beast to turn with her, whipping its massive tail into her path.

The charging raptor sailed through the air, dead before she hit the mossy water, her spine broken, chest cavity crushed.

Only then did the spinosaur accept its condition, leaning forward and collapsing into the shallows. It drew one massive, gurgling breath, sputtered a fountain of crimson, and lay still.

It would not take long for the scavengers and carrion-eaters to discover the enormous kill and come sniffing around. Loana knew her tribe would soon arrive, to carve up the beast and secure the meat back in their impressive network of caves. For the moment, she was content to stagger to the dead raptor, fall to her knees in the muck and mud, and cry silently as the two younger dinosaurs circled them, nosing and nudging the carcass, to no avail.

The mother raptor's name was Daisy. Loana had saved her hatchlings left for dead by the rampaging tyrannosaur which had killed an AEGIS survey party six years previous. The very survey party that Loana's mother and father had led. She remembered Daisy wasn't sure about her at first, but when this young human began to apply skilled first aid, nursing them back to health, a slow trust began to build. Eventually two of the three hatchlings recovered.

"Luanne Baxter" was sixteen when the tyrannosaur shattered the picket wall and thundered through the surveyor encampment, snapping up her father in its powerful jaws, crushing her mother under clawed, sinewy feet and legs. She saw her father, bloody and perforated in that huge bear trap of a mouth, thrusting his camp knife into the beast's right eye before the top half of him dropped to the grassy hill. Three other members of the survey crew tried to fight back, each torn in half by those savage, dagger teeth. By the time the pounding footfalls passed and Luanne crept tentatively from her hiding place in the hollow of a dead tree, she could see that the job had been thorough. Not one of the surveyors was left alive.

In point of fact, there wasn't much in the way of remains to be buried. The crew's temporary shelters lay in shreds, every weapon either bent in half or emptied of ammunition, with no spare cartridges to be found. She managed to salvage her father's camp knife, and fill a pack full of sundry first aid supplies and some clothes. A dented canteen, and a half-finished map that had been drawn by her mother rounded out her haul. And only then, standing atop that rise, where the crew had been certain they'd be safe from any carnivorous predators, gazing around at the blood streaked grass and broken tents...

She wept.

This wasn't a bad dream—it was real, it had happened. She was a teenage orphan in a strange, wild, and primal land. She was marooned in the Hollow Earth. If she wanted to survive she would have to find a safer "home base". Someplace much higher up, perhaps in the mountains to the south and west, which was incidentally the same direction the T-rex had gone. Figuring this apex predator was both easy to track and tended to clear everything in its path, she decided to follow it, working her way toward the mountains.

She came across the raptors the following morning, arriving at the aftermath of a brutal encounter. Daisy lay wounded at one end of the clearing, while three new hatchlings tried to hide in the dappled jungle sunlight. The tyrannosaur had bulldozed straight through the clearing, crushing two unhatched but viable eggs in addition to the damage to the mother and one of the three hatchlings.

Luanne set about trying to help the baby raptor first, soon discovering its back had been broken. It didn't survive the night. Some compresses of clay mud and moss helped soothe the mama raptor's flesh wounds, and the time spent growing accustomed to the strange human—with whom her offspring quickly bonded—eased her natural mistrust. Truth be told, Luanne knew that had the mother not been injured, she would have attacked and probably killed the teenager out of defensive instinct.

It was three days before Daisy could walk again, and Luanne stayed with the raptors the entire time, befriending the young ones, caring for the mother's wounds, sharing water from her canteen which was quickly emptied.

Within the course of a week, this awkward teen from the surface world had lost a family, and then gained a new one. A hesitant three-some of what would eventually be called Utahraptors—though those particular fossils wouldn't be discovered on the surface world for another half-century.

Luanne and her raptor family followed the shoreline of what the surveyors termed the Dinosaur Coast, toward some high ground and the apparently active thermal vent in some distant mountains. For several weeks, she kept herself and her little pack of dinosaurs hidden and safe in the steamy jungle, slowly working their way toward the mountains, venturing out only to hunt small game. The young raptors were especially fond of helping with a kill, and were easily trained in group hunting strategy, of which Daisy approved. By the time they encountered other humans, Luanne could ride Daisy as a mount, and was training the rapidly-growing juveniles likewise.

She eventually got used to this odd world, with its stifling heat and constant, immobile sun. As her parents had explained prior to their grisly demise, this was a large, subterranean world, echoing the surface world and yet standing apart from the passage of time. It was a place of primeval beauty and danger, dominated by a colossal inland sea, hemmed in by mountains that climbed high into the clouds and haze of the sky above. Occasionally, she'd spot a sail far away on the water, or strange creatures in the distance. But none of them showed up in her quarter of the Dinosaur Coast, so she paid them no heed.

After almost three months alone with her raptor pack, she surprised a small hunting party of what appeared to be homo sapiens, bodies painted with lime and ash, carrying Stone Age slings and spears. Using a dash of guile with an overall natural charisma, she brilliantly parlayed their surprise at her raptor rapport into their complete patronage. They were called the People of Red Mountain, owing to the hue of their cave homes, and they accepted Luanne as "Loana", a sort of living goddess. A primitive but powerful symbiosis blossomed.

The Red Mountain tribe taught her their rudimentary spoken tongue, as well as their system of hand signs—useful when hunting or being hunted. She taught them English. They took her to impressive vantage points in the southern peaks and cliffs, the highest of which remained unscalable, extending upward into the clouds before disappearing from sight. She traveled west as far as the Mammoth Peninsula, and east to where the barren Razor Coast met the deep blue Hades Expanse, where a massive volcano chugged ash and smoke into the sultry sky. She filled in her mother's map along the way.

With her new family, she traversed throughout what her people called the Jungles of Madness, teaching them new hunting methods, ways to go after larger game, and how to improve their home compound. An underground aquifer was tapped for use inside one of the large communal caverns, the cool water piped in with bamboo plumbing. Better hygiene reduced disease, and modern first aid techniques ensured a higher birthrate and lower infant mortality. The ranks of the Red Mountain tribe swelled.

Granted, they always lost some of their number to dangerous dinosaur predators, or encounters with the giants and their domesticated mammoth herds. But for the most part, the Red Mountain people thrived, with Loana and her hunting pack as their chief asset.

But now the pack was reduced by one. Daisy had sacrificed herself to give Loana and the young raptors a chance to live.

In this sweltering, primeval world, it was truly kill or be killed.

Quiet tears streaked down Loana's cheeks. She could hear the squawking of pteranodons circling above, eager for an easy meal. And suddenly, there it was: the musk of her fellow hunters, combined with the lime and ash body paint with which her people adorned themselves.

The salvage party numbered a dozen able hunters, armed with flint-tipped spears and double-headed axes of chipped volcanic glass. They would dismantle the spinosaur carcass in a matter of a few minutes, retreating back through the jungle pass to the safety of their home among the caves and mountains. The meat would feed the entire tribe, and the local scavengers would still get a meal out of the bargain.

They would not butcher Daisy. The raptor matriarch would lie where she fell, food for the scavengers and insect life. The tribe would eat so well from the spinosaur that it was never in question.

As the salvage crew approached, Loana tried to stand, and realized her ankle had twisted in the fall. The pain was only now reaching her, so preoccupied she'd been with Daisy's demise.

Spot nudged his muzzle under Loana's arm, helping to steady her, as Mabel, the juvenile female, padded around to her other side. Loana hobbled back onto the grass as the carvers got to work.

All except one.

Yorg was a young hunter of roughly Loana's years, proud and painted like the others, with dark hair, and piercing gray eyes that seemed to smile no matter his outward expression. His left shoulder and bicep were puckered from where an opportunistic smilodon had caught him off-guard. But then, all smilodons were opportunistic. Loana had supervised his recovery, which led to a deep bond between them.

In generations past, that wound would have been fatal. In this case, Yorg was the beneficiary of all that Loana brought to the table: quick thinking intellect, basic hygiene, and a soft yet firm touch. She'd deftly sewn Yorg's wounds, giving him herbal sedatives for the pain. He'd recovered fully in half the time most would have taken to die, further cementing Loana's reputation among her people—and Yorg's absolute adoration.

The young man saw Loana hobbling between the two remaining raptors and approached quietly as the butchers worked on the spinosaur behind him. He knew to fear such beasts in the wild, and even these answered only to the outlander. He closed the distance, stopping just a few paces shy of the trio to allow the raptor guardians to smell him and acknowledge his status as one of the tribe.

"You are hurt," he said in a soft baritone.

She blinked through teary eyes. "I am."

"What can I do?" he asked.

Loana grunted pensively. "Do you remember how I showed you to set a broken nose?"

Yorg sighed, nodding. Gently placing a thumb on either side of the bridge of her crooked appendage, he lowered his own head to kiss the top of hers. There was an abrupt *crack*, a small gush of blood, and Loana gripped the back of Yorg's neck with her right hand, groaning through her teeth, but not letting any signals of true distress reach her reptilian guardians. She didn't want them to injure the young man in her defense.

Two hunters came over to the group with offerings of raw meat and viscera for the raptors. While they buried their snouts in the feast, Yorg gave Loana a boost up to Spot's back, taking her weight off the bad ankle, and putting it in a better place to examine.

Using his fingers to gingerly probe the swollen flesh around her lower leg, he determined it wasn't broken, and produced a thin roll of leather and some rawhide ties from his hunting pack to wrap the injured foot with.

With slabs of fresh spinosaur meat wrapped in tanned hides, the hunters departed from the wetlands and into the jungle pass, an area clear enough to provide passage safe from the carnivorous plants and giant insects which prowled the deep rainforest. Yorg walked at the head of the column, next to

Loana, who sat astride Spot. Mabel trotted apace with her brother, trilling at Loana as she occasionally nuzzled her surrogate mother's thigh.

They were less than a mile into their trek when a shadow flashed over Spot's back, and Loana craned her head over her shoulder to look, squinting at the unmoving sun at their backs. Pteranodons circled overhead. That meant the scavengers had been driven away from the remains they'd left behind. Driven away, perhaps, by a larger scavenger?

"We need to hurry," Loana quietly warned.

"I know," Yorg replied under his breath, "but we can't move any faster." He turned, striding backward as he did a silent head-count of the hunters laden with wrapped spinosaur meat.

A roll of thunder rumbled up from the wet-lands through the jungle pass.

No. Not thunder.

The footfall of something heavy. Followed by a roar that sounded like a diesel freight train blaring its horn and grinding its brakes along the tracks simultaneously.

Loana tensed and her expression clouded over. She knew that roar. Although most tyrannosaurs sounded alike, she'd spent enough time in this one's territory to know it from any other.

"Spears," she grunted.

"You're hurt," Yorg protested. "I will fight."

Loana locked his eyes with her own and spoke firmly. "Give. Me. My. Spears."

There was no adequate protest. Yorg led Spot and Loana to the side of the marching column, Mabel following closely behind. He procured one of the long, flint-tipped spears from a grizzled, middle-aged tribesman, who resisted at first, but immediately gave up and offered it over when Loana shot him the look she'd just given Yorg. Her javelins arrived with a young apprentice hunter, who bowed at the waist as he handed them to her.

She knew very well she wasn't in the best fighting shape, after her earlier altercation with the spinosaur. Her right ankle was twisted and tender, and that was her bracing foot. It would throw off her spear distance and accuracy. She had a throbbing sinus pain around her puffy nose, and realized they would be facing into the sun, while it would be at the rex's back. She was also down one of her punch gauntlets.

Then a copse of palm trees exploded in shreds of green fronds and wood pulp, and the tyrannosaur—the venerable one-eyed beast that had destroyed a surface world survey team and feasted on her parents—thundered into the jungle pass.

The party scattered toward the relative safety of the rainforest on either side. There were no screams of terror, not yet anyway. Just the heavy breaths of running men laden with precious cargo.

The rex tilted its head to take in the scattering humans before it, seeing only through its left eye, thanks to Loana's father. It was a huge beast, almost four meters at the shoulder and over twelve meters from snout to tail. It strode hunched over, its gargantuan hips as the fulcrum point of its enormous frame. The blood caked around its scaly mouth and nostrils indicated it had already partaken of the spinosaur's remains, and had tracked the smell of its meat to this traveling butcher shop.

Once again it bellowed, that train horn reverberating through the valley. The sky above the jungle canopy came alive with every variety of flying thing. The rex took an aggressive first step, then another. Darting its massive head into a thicket of vines, its jaws clamped shut and it drew back, the legs of a lone hunter flailing silently outside its mouth. Once again the jaws snapped open and closed, crushing the rest of the tribesman with those impossibly cruel teeth.

Loana clicked her tongue, and Mabel trotted to her side. The dinosaur huntress extended her left hand and gently caressed the neck of the raptor, nodding to Yorg as she did so.

"Climb up," she instructed.

Yorg frowned. "I'm not ready."

"You're ready," Loana insisted. "Climb up now."

The rex stomped to the other side of the pass, snatching up another hunter from the brush, tossing the dismembered body and its innards across the open trail.

It's not even hungry, Loana thought, narrowing her eyes. *It's just killing to punish us for trespassing in its territory.* She gripped the long spear in her right hand, the two remaining javelins sticking up from the woven harness on her back.

"We need to take the fight to it now," she told Yorg. "While it's distracted by the meat."

Yorg looked a bit green astride Mabel's haunches. He'd seen Loana do impressive things while standing on the backs of her raptors, and he knew that was not for him. Not now, not yet. He'd do well merely to stay mounted while using his own spear, yet he wanted desperately to impress the Red Mountain patron of the hunt. His head began to swim. Before he knew what he was doing, he'd already nudged Mabel's flank with his leather-wrapped feet and was off like a shot.

Loana's eyes grew wide as she watched Mabel charge toward the tyrannosaur, Yorg gripping his spear like a mounted knight with a lance. Giving Spot a soft kick with her own heel, she took off after him.

The tyrannosaur stopped in mid-bite, watching their approach, gore pooling and dripping from its maw.

The two raptors charged, each hugging an opposite side of the pass, forcing the rex to turn its head back and forth to see each of them properly. The pain from Loana's ankle radiated up through her leg, and the headache from her freshly-set nose almost gave her double vision as she rode into the unmoving glow of sunlight.

Yorg leaned forward to lower his center of gravity and make it easier to stay on Mabel's back. He choked back on the haft of the spear and prepared to make the most of what was hopefully a well-placed throw.

Only meters away now.

Loana goaded Spot with her right foot out of habit, and the wave of agony from her ankle hit like a brick wall. The edges of her vision danced with darkness. She blinked, watching as Mabel carried Yorg directly under the rex's left side. There was a human battle cry, and as the spear found its mark in the belly of the beast, the sound made way to the familiar bellow of the diesel train. Anticipating the tail-whip as the massive rex turned away from their charge, Mabel jumped, clearing the serpentine appendage by mere centimeters.

But unlike the other large prey they'd hunted, the rex's tail wound back on itself, recoiling at Yorg's head height, and the snap launched him forward. He rocketed off Mabel's back and into the scrub, silent and immobile.

Mabel slowed her pace and turned, heading back toward the spot where Yorg's unconscious body had come to rest. She nuzzled at his shoulder, but her rider did not move.

Loana tensed. All the game she'd stalked and hunted, large and small, had led her to this showdown with the rex that had killed her parents, and was now trying to slaughter her adoptive people. The one-eyed, barrel-headed monster that existed only to kill at its whim.

One-eyed.

That was it!

Thank you, Papa.

Pressing her heels into Spot's ribcage, she slowed and broke off her attack, the raptor sprinting out of harm's way as the rex snapped at the air behind them. Signaling the hunters in the brush, she raised her long spear and let loose a warbling war cry with flickering tongue. Gingerly, she pushed herself up to a standing position on Spot's back, raising both hands and repeating the call, as Spot kept pace just out of range of the rex's injured stride. Every step the raptor took was agony for the woman standing atop its back and hips. But she screamed her scream of vengeance, even as her right leg threatened to crumple beneath her, and the merciless sun baked every living thing in the pass.

The ash-painted faces of primitive hunters emerged from the low jungle opposite Loana all along the pass, raising their spears and mimicking her cry. Even Yorg, freshly conscious and head still swimming, stumbled to his feet with the aid of Mabel.

The tyrannosaur stopped in its tracks and turned toward the sound erupting from the jungle behind it. Lowering its head, it bellowed bloody rage at the painted humans mocking it from the rainforest. It raged back and forth, not knowing where to strike.

"Spot, now."

A single tap from the butt of the long spear was all the signal the raptor needed to charge. Rider and mount flew across the open plain, Loana crouched in her surfing stance. She gripped the spear and readied her thrust. There would only be one chance at this.

One final war cry, as they closed with the great rex. Then she saw it start to turn its head, its one good eye scanning in her direction.

"Unh," she grunted, and Spot leaped, a sinewy mass of claws and fury. Loana pushed off with her wounded foot, pain arcing through her entire leg. Both hands remained on the spear, its flint point trained on the single reptilian eye.

She came down on the tyrannosaur's left shoulder, spear plunging downward into the soft eye socket, then carving upward through the tissues of the skull as her weight came down around its neck. Her savage cry of vengeance merged with the freight train roar of the dying rex.

Spot tore open its abdomen and launched away before the snapping jaws could find a target. One by one, the Red Mountain tribesmen began to emerge from the brush and encircle the rex, spears at the ready.

Gasping for breath in the sweltering air, Loana let go her grip on the spear and slid from the dinosaur's shoulder, falling with the beast, curling into the hollow of its left flank, unconscious.

There were a few twitches from the monstrous extremities, then the rex lay completely still, the hunter with it.

Two of the Red Mountain tribesmen lifted Loana to Spot's back, as Yorg returned from the end of the caravan astride Mabel. Once again, the butchers made busy with the carcass.

As the two dinosaur riders loped up the jungle pass toward their mountain home, Loana drifted in and out of consciousness, her face wet with the sweat from her mount's neck, and her own. She knew she wouldn't be able to hunt for a while. Recovery for both riders and mounts would take some time. But at least some sense of vengeance had been satisfied.

And perhaps, most importantly, her people would not go hungry.

ABOUT THE AUTHORS

COLIN FISK has been publishing stories and games for more than thirty years. Though best known as one of the writers and designers of the original *Cyberpunk* RPG, he's worked on more than ten published games as well as various supplements. When he's not writing or working at his day job in the technology world, he can be found speaking at conventions, watching movies, taking photos, or cooking with ingredients from his garden. Colin lives in Reno, Nevada, with his wife and fellow author, Margaret McGaffey Fisk, and their four cats.

PAUL J. HOWARD has spent more years than he cares to admit embracing a bad case of creative ADD, flitting between songwriting, acting, animation and even commercial art and product design (*offworldpercussion.com*). After helping his wife, the author Ginger G. Howard, edit her first two novels, his competitive streak kicked in and now, he is knee-deep toiling away at his very first novel. Of course, because he also has a bad case of the "Ooh, shiny"s, his sprawling sci-fi epic keeps getting interrupted by each new idea. Thus, his entry here. Enjoy.

ROSE LAMONT comes from a literary family and is a lifelong writer of fiction of all kinds, including the novels *Chasing Stardust* and *Chasing Skies*. Born and raised in the city, she now lives in rural Washington state.

R.L. PACE has had a widely diversified career ranging from circus ringmaster and radio broadcaster to financial planner and rocket fuel researcher. That rich background has served as a springboard and catalyst for his writing, which in addition to this contribution, includes the novels of the *Rising Son* trilogy, essays, short stories, and political commentary. He lives with his wife, cat, and dog in the Puget Sound area of Washington State.

MARTIN SHANNON has been using his imagination to avoid weeding since he was in short pants. His first series, *Tales of Weird Florida*, is an homage to the Sunshine State he knows and loves, and spent countless hours riding his bike through as a kid. It's got mystery, mayhem, and more than a little Magick. He hopes you enjoy the supernatural side of the upside down state, but if not, he's got a banjo, and he knows how to use it. You can find out more at *martin-shannon.com*.

JAMES STUBBS is a longtime game designer and author of fiction under various pseudonyms. He served as line producer on the popular 1PG roleplaying games from Deep7 Press, authoring many supplements in addition to publishing original and licensed material under his own Heyoka Studios imprint. He also contributed to material to the *Airship Daedalus* roleplaying game. A die-hard pulp fan and aficionado, James lives in Darlington, South Carolina.

A mad scribbler of art and fiction, BRINA WILLIAMSON spends her days hunched over a drawing table or keyboard, developing her skills and habitual bad posture. Her stories always seem to end up finding their way to a 1920s–1940s setting or theme, and Brina has happily embraced the vintage genre, primarily writing cozy mysteries and pulp adventures. *Merona Grant and the Lost Tomb of Golgotha* was her first full length novel, and venture into the pulp adventure genre, and it quite clearly won't be her last, as she is soon to release a Merona Grant prequel and has plans for several more sequels to follow. Her website is *brinawilliamson.com*.

TODD DOWNING has written extensively for stage, screen and tabletop adventure games over the past thirty years, with some half-dozen published novels and three fiction anthologies to his credit. He is the original creator of the AEGISverse, having written the comics and radio dramas that everything in the setting is based on. You can connect with him at *todddowning.com,* and keep up to date with *Airship Daedalus* and the AEGISverse at *airshipdaedalus.com.*

Other AEGISverse content available:

A Shield Against the Darkness
Assassins of the Lost Kingdom (by E.J. Blaine)
The Golden City
Legend of the Savage Isle
The Arctic Menace
Raiders of the Red Storm
AEGIS Tales volume 1
Airship Daedalus volume I (the original comic strips)
Airship Daedalus Radio Adventures 1 & 2
AEGIS Tales Radio Adventures 1 – 4
Airship Daedalus Retro Pulp Adventure RPG
AEGIS Field Manual (RPG sourcebook)
AEGIS Interplanetary Guidebook (RPG sourcebook)
Valley of the Mist (RPG sourcebook)
AEGIS Vigilante Team Resource Guide (RPG sourcebook)
Under the Surface (RPG sourcebook)